That's Ghosts for You

13 Scary Stories

That's Ghosts for You

13 Scary Stories

Edited by
Marianne Carus

Illustrated by
YongSheng Xuan

Front Street / Cricket Books

Chicago

To my nephew Zhuan Xuan
—Y. S. X.

"Mary Jo and the Hairy Man" by Eric A. Kimmel, © 2000 by Eric A. Kimmel "The Night of the Weeping Woman" by Mary Kay Morel, © 2000 by Mary Kay Morel "That's Ghosts for You" by Susan Price, © 2000 by Susan Price "The Glashtyn" by Josepha Sherman, © 2000 by Josepha Sherman

Grateful acknowledgment is made to the following for permission to reprint the copyrighted material listed below.

Rebecca Armstrong for "The Haunting of the Pipes" by Gerry Armstrong from October 1982, Vol. 10, No. 2 *Cricket* magazine, © 1982 by Gerry Armstrong. Deepa Agarwal for "The Airi" by Deepa Agarwal from October 1999, Vol. 27, No. 2 *Cricket* magazine, © 1999 by Deepa Agarwal. Dell Publishing, a division of Random House, Inc., for "Triple Anchovies" by Marion Dane Bauer, © 1992 by Marion Dane Bauer from *Funny You Should Ask* by David Gale, editor. Robert D. Culp for "A Place of Haunts" by Robert D. Culp from October 1978, Vol. 6, No. 2 *Cricket* magazine, © 1978 by Robert D. Culp. Frank O. Dodge for "Bones" by Frank O. Dodge from July 1995, Vol. 22, No. 11, and August 1995, Vol. 22, No. 12 *Cricket* magazine, © 1995 by Frank O. Dodge. Nancy Etchemendy for "Bigger than Death" by Nancy Etchemendy from March 1998, Vol. 25, No. 7 *Cricket* magazine, © 1998 by Nancy Etchemendy. Juanita Havill for "The Mysterious Girl at the Pool" by Juanita Havill from August 1991, Vol. 18, No. 12 *Cricket* magazine, © 1991 by Juanita Havill. Kathleen M. Muldoon for "A Ghostly Game of Puckeen" by Kathleen M. Muldoon from October 1999, Vol. 27, No. 2 *Cricket* magazine, © 1999 by Kathleen M. Muldoon. Aaron Shepard for "The Man Who Sang to Ghosts" by Aaron Shepard from June 2000, Vol. 27, No. 10 *Cricket* magazine, © 2000 by Aaron Shepard.

Library of Congress Cataloging-in-Publication Data
That's ghosts for you: thirteen scary stories/edited by Marianne Carus; illustrated by YongSheng Xuan.—1st ed.
p. cm.
Summary: An international collection of spine-tingling stories, including such titles as "Bigger than Death," "The Airi," and "The Man Who Sang to Ghosts."
ISBN 0-8126-2675-3
1. Ghost stories. 2. Children's stories. [1. Ghosts—Fiction. 2. Short stories.] I. Carus, Marianne. II. Xuan, YongSheng, ill.
PZ5.T3135 2000
[Fic]—dc21   00-055094

Contents

Preface

I'VE ALWAYS WANTED to see a ghost. Years ago we took our young children to England and stayed in several ancient castle hotels. One of these, complete with secret underground passages and its own resident ghost (according to the hotel guide), sounded especially attractive. We arrived late and were guided through long, dark hallways that were lined with suits of armor standing at attention. They looked like medieval knights—almost alive! Were there ghosts hiding inside?

After we settled down in our bedrooms and our kids were asleep, I got up again. It was close to midnight. We had been promised a ghost, and a ghost I was going to find, on my way to the washroom. Goose bumps rose on my arms and neck when I heard a clock strike twelve times. Where was that ghost?

I finally reached the washroom, turned on the light switch next to the door, and was shocked to see wild American wallpaper depicting bath toys and other ordinary, entirely prosaic pictures in the most glaring colors. Enough to scare away any ghost or spook or even a poltergeist. The eerie mood was gone. Sad to say, I did not see a ghost on that trip to England and I *still* haven't seen one.

But I love to read and collect ghost stories—scary ones that make you imagine the rattling of chains and hear groans and sighs that raise the hairs on the back of your neck. Several of the stories in this book were written for *Cricket* magazine and were published some time ago. Others are brand new and will appear in *Cricket* in the near future. And several were written especially for this book, by such famous authors as Susan Price and Eric A. Kimmel. In the true *Cricket* tradition there are ghost stories from all over the world. You'll read about a Japanese bard who sings to ghostly samurai warriors. A well-known Indian author, Deepa Agarwal, writes about the frightful *airi*, a ghost who makes people lose their minds with her jingling silver anklets.

There are friendly and helpful ghosts, desperate ghosts, and phantoms who like to destroy things and frighten people. But not all ghosts have human shapes. You'll read about a set of enchanted bagpipes from Scotland whose master was killed while leading the Highlanders into battle playing his pipes. "And only I shall play them—ever!" he had sworn. There is a ghost dog who has a very special reason for befriending a dog-crazy brother and sister. And on and on.

Start reading—and let those goose bumps rise all over your body (it's delicious!)—then write to me and let me know which story you enjoyed most. That's ghosts for you!

—Marianne Carus
Editor in Chief
Cricket magazine

That's Ghosts for You

13 Scary Stories

Bigger than Death

Nancy Etchemendy

JOSIE AND I wanted a dog more than anything else on Earth. We wished for one every time we threw pennies in a fountain or watched the evening star drop behind the trees. At night, after Mom and Dad had gone to bed, Josie'd sneak out her bedroom window, and I'd sneak out mine, and we'd sit together on the roof and talk about dogs.

"You're so dumb, Jake," Josie would say. "Bulldogs are creepy."

"Hah. Golden retrievers are creepy," I'd say.

We had this ongoing argument about what our ideal dog would be. But it didn't really matter—any dog would do, as long as it had a tail to wag and a friendly face.

Sure, Josie and I are twins, and we like each other

and all that stuff. But we get sick of each other sometimes, too. If we had a dog, there'd always be somebody
to hang out with, even when we wished we'd never
heard the word "sibling."

One summer night, as we sat together on the roof,
Josie saw something. "What's that?" She pointed down
toward a dark shadow on our driveway. The moon
was up, and everything looked either black or milky.
At first all I saw was darkness. Then the shadow
moved, and I thought I heard the jingle of metal.

"Did you see that? What is it?" Josie crouched at
the edge of the roof with her nightgown hiked up
around her knees. The shadow flowed out onto the silvery gravel of the drive and whined softly.

For one astonished second, Josie and I just stared
at each other. Then we scrambled down onto the
porch. There in our yard stood a dog. A big black dog
with long, shaggy hair—like a dream come true.

Josie made a little kissing noise and held out her
hand. I said, "Here, boy." And the dog came to us
slowly, taking a few steps forward, then a step back,
not sure whether to trust us, I guess.

When he was close enough to pet, I put my arms
around his neck and let him lick my face. He had that
great doggy smell that always makes me think of dirt
and grass and piles of leaves.

"Don't say, 'Here, boy,' you moron," said Josie.
"She's a female."

"Oh," I said, pulling back and looking. "I wonder
what her name is."

I felt for her collar while she sat patiently, whuffing

hot breath on my cheek as Josie scratched her ears. I was almost glad when I found no tags, just a silver choke chain with a small rusty bell on it.

"I bet she's hungry," said Josie, stroking the dog's flank. "I can feel her ribs."

I ran my hand through her fur. The dog was so skinny you could just about feel every bone, and her coat was tangled and full of dirt. If she belonged to someone, they weren't taking very good care of her.

"What can we give her?" I said. That was sort of a problem. Our mom's a vegetarian, which means we don't exactly eat the kind of stuff dogs dream of. I thought about the leftovers from dinner—a moderately disgusting mixture of brown rice, tofu, and broccoli. I couldn't imagine any self-respecting dog, even a starving one, eating that. Then I had a thought. "Milk! I'll get her a bowl of milk."

So Josie waited with the dog, and I sneaked into the kitchen to fill one of Mom's mixing bowls with milk and a couple of raw eggs.

The dog lapped it up, but as soon as she finished, she trotted into the shadows and disappeared.

"Don't go!" Josie called after her as loudly as she dared. It was a warm night, and our parents' window was open. "Come back." But the dog was gone.

We sat on the porch steps awhile, hoping she'd return.

"I think she'll be back when she gets hungry again," I said. "Nobody else is feeding her."

"No duh," said Josie.

We smiled at each other in the moonlight, our

insides full of scrabbly excitement, like just before Christmas or our birthday. We were both thinking the same thing.

"We're going to have a dog!" I whispered.

"What's a good name?" said Josie.

The perfect name wrote itself in my mind. "Shadow!"

"Yeah! Shadow."

Of course, nothing ever goes exactly as planned. The next day, we piled together all the money we'd stashed from allowance and odd jobs. Eleven dollars and ninety-four cents. There would've been more, but we'd spent a lot on comics and candy and stuff. You know how it goes.

We had some trouble agreeing on how best to spend our limited funds. Dog food, of course. But what kind? The grocery store had lots, and we came home with two cans of Woof Buddies, a small bag of kibble, and a big package of beef tailbones that the guy at the meat counter practically gave us.

We brought the stuff home and hid it in various places, I guess because we were afraid Mom and Dad wouldn't approve if they knew we were feeding a stray. The bones were hardest to hide, because they had to be kept cold. But we have a gargantuan freezer in the garage, and it's got so much stuff in it that Mom never noticed our paper-wrapped package from the butcher.

That night, after our parents were asleep, we

sneaked downstairs. I got an old aluminum platter, and we put an assortment of goodies on it—kibble with some Woof Buddies mixed in and a couple of bones. We set the platter in the driveway and sat back to watch.

Shadow must've been hiding in the bushes watching *us,* because as soon as we set the platter down, we heard the jingle of her chain, and she appeared almost as if from nowhere. We hugged her and petted her and showed her the food. She sniffed it, drooling and licking her chops, but for some reason she wouldn't eat it.

"What's the matter?" asked Josie. "It's good for you."

Shadow looked at the platter, looked at us, and whined.

"Maybe she's shy," I said. "Maybe she doesn't want us to watch her eat."

"Yeah, well, she wasn't shy last night." Josie looked hurt. I mean, we had spent all our hard-earned cash on food for Shadow, and now the dog wouldn't eat it. Maybe I was a little hurt, too.

"Come on," I said. "Let's leave her alone and see what happens."

So we pretended to say good-night and went into the house. We tried to make it look like we were going to bed but stayed just inside the front door, opening it a crack so we could spy.

Shadow did something completely unexpected. She grabbed the platter in her mouth and dragged it away. By the time we ran back outside, she and the food were long gone. We couldn't find her anywhere.

When we fixed Shadow's dinner the next night, we used a paper plate. It was the same scene all over. The dog wouldn't eat until we hid. Then she dragged the food away, plate and all.

This went on a long time—four or five nights, maybe. One of the weirdest parts of the whole thing was that even though Shadow kept taking the food, she didn't seem to be putting on any weight. You could still feel her bones. If anything, she was getting even skinnier. Sometimes she almost seemed transparent. She was still warm, though, and her breath was still doggy and hot.

When Shadow was gone, Josie and I would come back out and search the bushes with no luck. Then we'd sit on the porch steps and listen to the crickets and the breeze, which somehow didn't sound as friendly as they used to, and try to figure out what was going on. On the night we put out the last of our dog food, we got such a bad case of the creeps that we ran inside and hid under our covers as soon as Shadow dragged her dinner away.

The next night, I got one of Mom's pie plates and filled it with milk and eggs, the only thing we could think of, since we had no more money for dog food. We set it in the driveway as usual and sat down to wait. But Shadow didn't come.

The moon got higher and higher. We waited with

nothing to do but jump every time we heard a leaf rustle or a twig snap. We thought we saw small, bright eyes peering at us from among the bushes.

Still the dog didn't come.

We must have fallen asleep there, because suddenly I felt as if I'd awakened from a dream. I sat up. The unmistakable jingle of Shadow's bell drifted through the night. The pie plate stood a few feet away, still full of milk and eggs, and Josie lay beside me, her breath soft and even.

I jiggled her shoulder. "Wake up, Josie. I hear Shadow!"

Still mostly asleep, Josie raised her head. "Huh?"

"It's Shadow!" I pointed to a patch of moving moonlight an arm's length away.

You can say I was crazy or dreaming, but I know what I saw. It was Shadow—I could smell her warm breath. But when I tried to touch her, my hand passed right through, and all I felt was a strange prickling, as if I'd rubbed my arm with a party balloon.

The sound of her bell was clear and real, though. She barked at us, whined, and ran back and forth.

I staggered to my feet, pulling Josie after me. "What is it, Shadow? What do you want?" I said.

She barked again, ran toward the bushes, and turned to see if we were following. Then she plunged into the thicket, still barking. I chased her through a wall of scratchy branches and out into the open field beyond.

"Wait up!" cried Josie. I could hear her far behind

me, but I was afraid if I slowed down, I might lose
Shadow forever. Tears trickled from my eyes, and the
wind blew them back along my face in chilly streaks.
I cried partly because the running hurt. It made my
lungs burn and my side ache. But I also cried because
somewhere deep down I knew I wasn't going to be
keeping Shadow. She'd never sleep beside my bed.
She'd never bark and skitter around me in circles
when I came home from school. She'd never swim in
the creek with me. Because something terrible had
happened, and part of me knew it.

She kept barking—sometimes that was the only
way I could keep track of her. We ran across the field,
darted between trees, threaded our way into another
thicket. There Shadow stopped and stood perfectly
still, panting and wagging her tail.

I was so out of breath that for a few seconds I had
to bend over and just gasp. I knew where we were.
Shadow had led me to the banks of the creek, a little
upstream from the place where Josie and I swam on
hot days. The bushes grew close together, and it was
the best hiding place I knew of. I could hear Josie
some distance behind, yelling at me to wait up.

Shadow looked around, whined, and disappeared
through a dark hole in the wall of leaves and branches.

"Shadow?" I called. "Where'd you go?"

I started to sweat. In a world where all the rules
about what's real and what's not seemed broken, I
knew that dark hole in the bushes was a place I didn't
want to enter.

Something soft and creepy touched my shoulder. I just about jumped out of my pants. "Ya-a-a-a-a-a!" I cried.

"Sheesh!" said Josie. "Lighten up. It's just me."

"Don't ever do that again!"

"What, touch you? Don't be a dweeb!"

"I'm not a dweeb. I'm just . . ."

Josie hugged herself and shivered. "I see what you mean. This place feels weird. Where's Shadow?"

I pointed toward the dark hole.

"No way I'm going in there," Josie said softly.

I closed my eyes and took a deep breath. "We'll go in together. You and me through thick and thin."

We had this tradition, you see, of linking arms and saying that whenever we were scared of doing something. I don't know why, but it seemed to make us braver. It was always easier to face stuff when we did it together. So we linked arms and walked into the dark undergrowth.

"Here, Shadow. Here, Shadow," I called, my voice shaky.

At first we heard nothing. Then a soft yipping came to our ears. We broke through into a little clearing and could hardly believe what we'd found.

At our feet lay a litter of four puppies, squeaking and climbing around on top of each other. Bones and paper plates littered their small nest. Mom's aluminum platter was there, and so was Shadow, cold and motionless. She'd been dead quite awhile, much too long to have led us there. We think she must've starved. She'd saved all her food for her puppies.

*   *   *

People ask us how we got our dog, Roofus. Well, that's the story. Roofus is one of Shadow's pups. We found homes for the other three, and they all live nearby.

So things ended well for everybody. Josie and I got our dog after all, and Shadow found help for her babies. It's true it's not a perfectly happy ending, but we did what we could. We buried Shadow under Mom's favorite rosebush and made a wooden marker, which Josie engraved. I like what it says:

"Here lies Shadow, whose love was bigger than death."

The Haunting of the Pipes
A Scottish Ghost Story

Gerry Armstrong

AN UNFRIENDLY WIND hissed around the tombstones of the graveyard and made thirteen-year-old Sandy shiver. It was Allhallows Eve. "Who ever would have thought that your love of bagpipes would lead us to this?" he called to his cousin Norman, forcing a laugh.

Norman turned. "Be quiet!" he whispered. "This is a funeral. Hold that end of the coffin higher. Let's get it over with."

They continued through the eerie darkness toward the new-dug grave.

It was not so much Norman's love of bagpipes that had brought them here, but his love of a bargain. A few days ago, the boys had noticed the bagpipe in

MacAlister's pawnshop window, marked at a ridiculously low price. They had mentioned it to their grandfather, and he had chuckled.

"Och, aye, that'll be the haunted bagpipe. MacAlister's hoping that the new generation won't have heard the story about Willie Wee."

"Who's Willie Wee?" both boys asked at once.

"Well, now . . ." Their grandfather settled back with the satisfaction of one who has a good story to tell. "Willie White was a gamekeeper who lived in this town in the early 1900s. He was a big, scowling man with red hair, and no one liked him because of the way he acted about his bagpipes. He'd never let another piper touch them. 'They're my own pipes,' he would declare, 'and only I shall play them—ever!'

"Well, World War I broke out, and Wee Willie White enlisted as a piper. It's a dangerous post, for it's the piper who leads the troops when they charge out of the trenches. On one charge, Willie Wee was killed. His pipes, however, were unharmed, so they were sent home to his brother, but he only kept them a few weeks before he sold them.

"I think every piper in town had Willie Wee's pipes at one time or another—and strange were the tales they told of noises in the night and ghostly apparitions. Willie had declared that no one else would ever play his pipes, and evidently he was making sure they wouldn't. The haunted pipes ended up in MacAlister's pawnshop, and he put them away for a generation. Then, in the forties, I heard that a piper named Jack Robertson had bought them.

"Jack was particularly proud of the trade he'd made that day for this fine set of pipes. 'They need to be fixed up,' he conceded, 'but they're good pipes.' Jack mixed glycerine and honey and then rubbed it well into the inside of the bag. He brushed off the accumulation of dust, wet the drones, and assembled the pipes again.

"Then he tried for five long hours to get those pipes in tune. Finally his wife, Jeannie, with her hands over her ears, cried, 'Will you stop before I lose my mind! You've been fooling with that thing for a time and a time!'

"Jack threw the pipes down on the couch. 'It's beyond my ken! I can't get them tuned to save my soul. Here it's midnight already; let's go to our bed.'

"So they did, but Jeannie couldn't sleep. All that tuning had given her a headache. 'A nice cup of tea should put me right,' she decided. She got up and started for the kitchen. As she passed the living room, she saw a man there, bending over the couch. She scurried back to the bedroom. 'Jack! Jack!' she gasped. 'There's a strange man in the house!'

"Jack jumped out of bed, ran into the living room, and snapped on the light. Then he called, 'Jeannie, you're imagining things. There's no one here.'

"Jeannie returned, peering around suspiciously, but the room was empty. 'But I saw him plain as plain,' she protested. 'Bending over the couch he was—a big, scowling, red-headed man. He wore old-fashioned gamekeeper's leggings, and his clothes were muddy or bloody.'

"Now it was Jack's turn to look frightened. 'Jeannie, girl, you're describing Willie Wee. It's a ghost you've seen. No wonder the pipes were such a bargain; they're haunted. Och! I'll get rid of the unchancy things tomorrow.'

"And he did. As before, the pipes eventually ended up in the pawnshop. And evidently, they're still haunted, if MacAlister's asking such a low price for them," their grandfather concluded.

The boys were silent for a while, pondering this strange tale.

"I feel sorry for Willie Wee," Sandy said. "It must be awful to be unable to play your real pipes. Too bad we can't kill his bagpipe for him. Then the ghost of Willie Wee could play the ghost of his pipes and be content."

"If the bagpipes were declared dead officially," Norman said thoughtfully, "if they were buried in the graveyard, then the ghost of Willie could take the ghost of the pipes—and the *real* pipes wouldn't be haunted anymore. Let's do it!"

"What do you think, Granddad?" Sandy asked.

Their grandfather looked troubled. "Well . . . I wouldn't have anything to do with a ghost if I were you, boys. I've heard of people turning gray overnight or losing the power of speech or becoming gibbering idiots from fright of ghosts."

But Norman was sure his plan would work. They pooled their savings and bought the bargain bagpipe from MacAlister that afternoon of Halloween.

So here they were now with Willie Wee's bagpipe in a pine box tied up with black ribbons. They had dug the grave that afternoon, but Norman had insisted that they must bury the pipes at midnight to be sure the ghost would be around.

Losh, it was dark! Sandy's hands felt clammy, and he wished the wind wouldn't make that moaning sound.

"Stop here," ordered Norman as they reached the grave.

Suddenly, a white form rose out of the open grave. With a scream, Sandy dropped the coffin.

"Wheest! It's only a cat," Norman scolded. "Since when have you been afraid of cats?"

"Well, I didn't know what it was at first," apologized Sandy, still shaking.

"I hope we didn't damage the bagpipe when we dropped it," Norman said. He untied the black ribbons, opened the coffin, and by the fitful light of the moon examined the bagpipe carefully.

"It's all right," he said, relieved. He replaced it and tied up the box again. Then he jumped down into the grave. "Hand me the coffin, Sandy." Norman set it down gently, climbed out again, and the boys pushed the dirt over the "dead" bagpipe.

They stood motionless by the grave. It was very cold. "Let's go," Sandy whispered.

"I wonder if Willie's ghost has got the bagpipe's ghost yet," mused Norman.

Sandy gripped Norman's arm. "Norman, *please.*"

"Not yet. We have to dig up my bagpipe," Norman reminded him.

"Let's just leave it. I'm afraid," said Sandy.

"You ninny," scolded Norman. "I'm not going to bury my bagpipe and leave it to rot."

"It's not your bagpipe, it's Willie Wee's," insisted Sandy.

"Stop talking and dig," commanded Norman.

Sandy was scared, but he was more afraid of going home alone, so he helped Norman dig. They dragged the coffin out of the hole, and Norman began to pull off the ribbons. Sandy got to his feet and stood, poised to go.

"Hurry, Norman," he pleaded. But his friend was kneeling as though turned to stone. The color was draining from his face, and his eyes were staring without understanding.

"Norman?" whispered Sandy again. He felt a cold sweat break out on his upper lip. Then the hairs rose on the back of his neck as he heard an unearthly sound. Bagpipe music—shrilling and moaning at their feet!

He couldn't remember making the decision to run. He just knew he was running—away from that ghostly music—through the graveyard, down the hill, across town, toward home. He flung himself onto the porch and leaned against the door, panting. His cousin was close behind him, and he, too, collapsed on the porch floor.

When he could speak, Sandy gasped, "Norman, what was it? What was in the box?"

Norman looked at Sandy and whispered huskily, "Nothing! The coffin . . . was . . . was . . . empty!"

And in the deserted graveyard, as the bloodless moon shone down on the empty coffin by the open grave, the thin trees danced to the haunting echo of pipe music.

A Place of Haunts

Robert Culp

FOR COTTON AND ME, Halloween was mostly a secondhand experience. We heard all manner of fearsome tales from the old folks and from our schoolmates in town. But we lived out in the hills, a far piece from the other kids, and our parents absolutely forbade us to go back into town on Halloween night. This year, however, Halloween came to us.

The last night of October promised to be a dark one; there was only the slimmest slice of a fingernail moon setting behind the oak trees. I was standing stock-still, trying to locate the hooty owl in the orchard, when Cotton slipped up and hooted in my ear.

"Thunderation, Cotton! You scared me skinny. You oughtn't to sneak up on people like that."

"I'm practicing for tonight, Rooster."

"Who you gonna scare? The pigs?" He knew as well as I did we were supposed to stick close to home.

"Want to get back at Garvey for trying to steal our honey and your pa's pigs?"

Now, technically, the old man hadn't tried either one of those schemes, but I thought it would be picky to say so. Garvey Bockenweiler was an old codger who lived alone just beyond the second ridge. Cotton and I figured him to be the meanest man this side of perdition. He had no use for people in general and kids in particular.

Pa wasn't so hard on Garvey, though he always warned us to steer clear of the old man's place. He said we must make allowances, but he didn't say why. For example, those things Cotton mentioned: Cotton and I found a bee tree, and Garvey came along and tried to take our honey. He didn't get it, but he tried. I thought that was pretty low, but Pa pointed out that if we had marked the tree ours, Garvey probably would have left it alone. Then there were the pigs. Every now and again Garvey caught and butchered one of our pigs. I figured that was stealing, but Pa said since the pigs ran wild, they weren't rightly ours. I didn't understand. For grownups, it was complicated. For us kids, it was simple; just the thought of that no-account varmint made us mad.

Did I want to get back at Garvey? Can a squirrel climb trees? Does a fish like water? "How?" I asked.

"Garvey's in town. I met him walking down the

trace before supper, clomping along in those heavy boots of his."

"So? Did you say boo or howdy?"

"You think I'm crazy? I hid in the bushes till he passed."

"Boy, I bet that scared him. Showed him not to mess with you."

Cotton gave me a look of pure exasperation. "Rooster, you want to hear my plan or not?"

"Shoot."

"When Garvey goes to the general store, he always hangs around past dark—just stands back in the corner and listens to folks talk."

"Yeah."

"And when he comes home, he takes the low trail through the pecan grove."

"Yeah."

"That's it, Rooster. I reckon we got about an hour before he comes traipsing home."

Of course I went along with it. The plan was downright perfect. It took three minutes to swipe a sheet from the laundry basket and an empty flour sack from the pantry. On the way across the ridge to the pecan grove, we broke off a middling-sized forked branch from a deadfall, and that was all we needed. With the sheet draped over the branch for a body, and the flour sack stuffed with leaves and tied tight to the fork for a head, we had the spookiest ghost that ever haunted a dark place.

The path Garvey took going home from town cut across the end of the pecan grove, just a short throw from the deep hole the ornery cuss had dug to catch pigs. Cotton and I figured it would be a good turnabout if we used that pig pit as our hiding place. When last we'd been by, he and I had tried to fill the hole with tree limbs; luckily the brush was still there, clogging up the pit. We climbed down just deep enough to hide us and our ghost—and waited.

Soon my teeth were rattling and my whole body was shivering, from excitement as much as from cold. It seemed as if we'd waited past midnight, but it couldn't have been an hour. Then, into the clearing came Garvey, stomping along in his heavy boots, mumbling to himself. When he was practically on top of us, Cotton let out a moan. There was dead silence. Garvey must have stopped like a balky mule.

"Who's that?" he quavered.

I groaned like a dying man. Garvey commenced stammering and backed away. Cotton and I let out a passel of wails and cries and raised our ghost as high as we could reach.

The old man bellowed, flung aside the sack of provisions he was toting, and lit out across the grove, leaving a trail of howls like a far-off train whistle.

Cotton and I tried to follow Garvey with our spook, but by the time we reached the edge of the woods, he was out of sight. There was no way to guess which direction he'd gone. We started home then, chortling and giggling like the half-wits we were.

"Ho, boy, Rooster. You reckon he'll ever stop?"

"Not till he's home safe and sound in that old shack of his," I said. "Hey, old Garvey makes pretty

good spook noises himself. Did you ever hear such a caterwauling?" I chattered on, never noticing Cotton had gone quiet.

"Hush, Rooster."

"Huh?"

"You hear that?"

We both froze and listened. Nothing. After a minute we walked on, and I started joshing Cotton about having spooks on the brain. Then it was my turn to be chilled full of goose bumps.

"Cotton! There's something behind us."

"You heard it, too?"

The rustling stopped. There was heavy breathing somewhere in the dark behind us. We turned around, but the thick brush hid everything. I touched Cotton. He was shaking worse than I was.

"Let's go," I whispered.

"I'm way ahead of you, Rooster." And he was.

With a real haunt on our tail, I dropped our fake spook and ran. The trail over the ridge toward my house was as black as the inside of a cave. Branches snagged our clothes and slapped our faces. In front, Cotton ran into every trifling limb on the path. Right behind him, I caught a powerful swat from the same dumb limbs as soon as he pushed past them. But neither of us complained. We could hear it following us, no doubt now—sticks snapping, brush swishing, dry leaves shuffling, and, on top of everything, that infernal throaty breathing.

We crossed a clearing at the crest of the ridge. Dark

as it was, we could see a little in the dim starlight. I grabbed Cotton's arm just as we plunged back into the trees.

"Wait," I hissed. "Let's rest a second. Maybe it'll lose our trail."

"Leggo," he panted. But he stopped with me.

The noise approached, then halted at the far side of the clearing. The perdicious breathing came in huge gasps now. The only other sound was my heart thudding like a tom-tom.

Then, in the gloom across the way, there appeared two pinpoint eyes like a pair of stars. Around them, I swear I could make out a monstrous form.

No need to say a word; Cotton was as scared as I was. We ran as if we were possessed. It was devil take the hindmost, and mostly I was the hindest. We forgot the trail and cut straight down the hill, bouncing from tree to bush, skidding over rocks, and thrashing through the brambles. All the while I fancied I could feel that beast breathing down my neck. I was near to giving up, when the light from my house came in sight. That gave me fresh hope, and I doubled my pace. I saw Cotton reach the porch and disappear inside the house. Escape was at hand.

Something seized my shirttail. My feet were still moving, but I wasn't going anywhere. I let out a bodacious screech and kicked and flailed like an unbroke horse. I heard my shirt rip, and then I was loose. In two hops I hit the kitchen door and busted into the house.

"Gracious, Rooster," said Ma with a big smile. "Were you two trying to give us a Halloween fright?"

Pa looked at my torn shirttail. "'Pears to me he's the one got the fright. Maybe he tangled with some ghost."

I gulped air while Ma and Pa chuckled at me. When I thought I could keep my voice from quivering, I said, "Aw, Pa, you know there's no such thing as ghosts."

Cotton and I were so all-fired happy to be safe from that place of haunts, we didn't mind the teasing. Cotton was afraid to go home through the dark, so we told Ma that his folks said he could stay over. We figured we could convince his folks later that it was just a misunderstanding. Anyway, we'd worry about that in the daylight.

Next morning before breakfast, Cotton and I eased out into the yard to check the scene. At the edge of the garden we spotted a strip of my shirttail snagged on the barbed wire.

"There, Rooster." Cotton pointed at the evidence. "You still say something grabbed you?"

It sure looked as if we'd imagined the whole thing. I walked toward the fence, feeling silly. Then I stopped.

"Cotton! Look at that."

Right near my snagged shirttail lay the sheet and the flour sack, folded as neat as fresh laundry. We ran over, and I grabbed them up as if they were certain proof that we weren't light in the head.

And there, in the soft dirt of the garden, leading in the direction of the pecan grove, was a trail of heavy boot tracks.

That's Ghosts for You
An English Ghost Story

Susan Price

*T*HIS IS A GHOST story from England, the country of ghosts. It happened in the early years of the last century, in the 1920s, in the town of Oldbury in Warwickshire. In those days Warwickshire policemen had black uniforms. Their black helmets had black badges, and their black jackets had black buttons. Even their whistles, on black chains, were black.

Why do I tell you this? What do you care about the uniforms of Warwickshire policemen? Because it's important to the story that you know this—though you won't know why until the end.

It's a true story. My father heard it from a man named Bill, who taught him his trade of repairing electrical motors. "I saw a ghost once," Bill said. "When I was about your age, about fourteen."

Of course, my father wanted to hear about the ghost. Bill told him the story many times, and later Dad told it to me.

It happened on a winter's night when a burned-out motor was brought into the works. The factory it came from wanted it back as soon as possible, so Jim McAtamnie was given the job of working through the night to rewind the coils. And Jim's apprentice, who would be helping him, was Bill.

They worked all day, stripping the burned coils from the motor and cleaning it up. At about six they went home with the other men to have their tea, but Jim took the works' keys with him, so he could let himself and Bill back in that evening.

So it was getting on for seven o'clock when Bill walked back to work by himself in the dark. Now we're so used to street lamps and lights in houses, bright headlights and brilliantly lit shop windows, that we forget how very dark it is at night when there's no moon and only the faintest spattering of stars.

The works was on the edge of Oldbury, where a long road led out into the country, and there weren't any streetlights. No houses, either, only factories, and they were locked and empty, with no lights. No cars on the road. You saw more horses and carts in those days than cars.

So Bill was walking down this long, dark road all

by himself, with nobody else in sight or hearing. And naturally his mind ran on ghosts, as it often does at such times.

There was a strong wind that night, too, and a lot of the ghost stories he knew had storms and strong winds in them. The wind screamed and thrashed the branches of trees, and the noise made him think of ghostly horses who screamed as they pulled ghost coaches.

And there was a gypsy girl, it was said, who'd drowned herself in a pool not far away. Her ghost roamed around the pool, hair and clothes dripping wet. Sometimes she screamed, too—he jumped at the next howl of wind. He tried to tell himself that the pool was too far away. She wouldn't bother coming this far. But who knew what a ghost might do?

At the entry to the works' yard, Bill stopped. From the other end of the entry came a regular banging, clapping noise. He couldn't think what it was, but his imagination showed him a huge, hulking brute of a man—or possibly some kind of goblin—crouching in the yard, banging a big club on the wall while it waited for Bill. When he came, it would raise the club high and . . .

Footsteps echoed in the entry, and Bill nearly ran away. A shape loomed from the darkness, and his heart lurched while his heels left the pavement with shock.

"That you, Bill?" said the shape. It was Jim, his hands in his pockets. "What's up?"

"Nothing," Bill said with relief. He felt quite unafraid now that he was with Jim and happily followed him through the entry, a low, arched tunnel of brick that smelled of dank, green water. Their feet splashed in puddles, and their footsteps echoed from the roof. Ahead of them that banging and clapping went on—but now, because he was with Jim, Bill knew it was only the door of their workshop blowing in the wind, banging to and fro.

The entry opened into a dark yard. The ground underfoot was rough, with half-buried bricks and broken cobblestones, and the only light came, dimly, from the doorway of the workshop. A gust of wind, a bang as the door slammed into its frame, and the light vanished. A moment later it reappeared as the door blew open and crashed against the wall.

They went in, and Jim stayed by the door for a moment to make sure it was shut against the wind.

It was a long, chilly building, full of darkness. The warmth seeped out through holes in the brickwork and gaps round the doors and windows, and piercing drafts blew about, snapping at the ears and ankles. The only light was at the far end of the shop, over the motor they were repairing. From the deep shadows overhead hung loops of oily rope and chain, dangling from the crane tracks. To either side iron shelves, loaded with drums of wire, emerged from the dark. There were faint shapes of tool racks and workbenches, vices and lathes. The whole place smelled of oil, with an underlying metallic tang, and whiffs of varnish. The smells grew stronger as Bill neared the motor, because the air was warmer there, softened by the old stove.

"There's some tea on the stove," Jim said, coming up behind him. The old enamel teapot sat on top of the stove most of the time.

"I had a bellyful at home," Bill said. "Let's get on."

They had to replace the motor's burned-out coils with new coils of wire. Jim threaded the wire through the slots in the motor and Bill "drew the wire through." That is, he took the wire and ran backward down the length of the shop, holding it in front of him and pulling it tight. He had to keep it as straight as he could so it wouldn't kink. When the wire was pulled tight, he went back to Jim, who threaded it through again and shaped the coil.

They went at it for hours. Again and again Bill ran backward from the little circle of light and the warmth of the stove into the chill darkness at the other end of the shop. His footsteps brought muffled echoes from the brick walls and the corrugated iron roof in the gloom above. When he reached the far end of the shop by the door, he was in darkness and could hear the wind biffing against the door and walls. Chilled by freezing drafts, he looked up the length of the shop and, far away, saw Jim stooping over the motor in the little circle of light, like someone on a lit stage in a dark, empty theater.

Then back up the shop he'd run, and with every step it would be warmer and lighter until he was back by the stove with Jim.

The wind outside never stopped rattling the door. Every now and again, it blew the door off its latch and slammed it into its frame and crashed against the wall. Strong, cold currents of air rushed through the shop. Jim would say, "Go and shut that door."

Bill would run to the door and fight to pull it shut against the wind, which struck cold against the sweat on his face and neck, making him shiver. Heaving the door shut, he firmly pressed the latch into place.

But the door blew open again. Why did it keep blowing open? Was it being opened by something other than the wind? Once that thought had occurred to Bill, it plagued him, just as thoughts of the gypsy girl's ghost had plagued him earlier.

That coldness that passed him by, prickling his skin—was it a draft, or was it a ghost? The darkness behind him that he ran into backward—was it empty? If he looked over his shoulder, what would he see? He snatched his head round, only to glimpse the shadowy racks of wire and tools.

"Don't twist the wire," Jim said.

The door end of the shop seemed lonely and dangerous—a long way from the light and from Jim, and much too close to the ill-fitting door and the dark, cold, windy night. Bill started to stop short of the door so he could run back to the light sooner. He tried not to—he would never have admitted being afraid to Jim—but it was as if his body had a mind of its own. "Far enough," his feet said. "It's too scary down here. Run back!"

"You're not pulling it tight enough," Jim said, and waved his hand to send him further back.

So Bill ran further back into the dark by the rattling door. It sounded as if someone was trying to open the door and couldn't—as if cold, stiff fingers couldn't quite manage the latch. His whole back prickled under his clothes. He was tensed for the touch of a wet, freezing hand that he was sure was coming. . . . With relief he went racing back to the circle of light.

Bill had a moment's rest, standing in the warmth and light while Jim shaped the coils. While he was standing there, the wind blew the door open again. It crashed against the wall and let in a strong gust of cold air.

"Go and see if you can't make that door stop shut," Jim said. His voice was muffled in all the space and silence of the big empty shop. "I'm sick to death of it."

Bill wanted to say, "Why don't you go and shut it?" But he was the boy, and Jim was the man. And Bill couldn't admit that he was afraid. So he started walking, slowly, down the length of the shop toward the racketing, banging door.

He was within a couple of feet of the door when he saw it. The door had blown open again, making a frame of darkness. At the center of that frame, hanging in midair, was a head. A face. A deathly white face, without a body, staring at him.

Bill's every joint locked. He couldn't run away; he couldn't move. His eyes stayed open and fixed on the thing outside the door. Somewhere deep inside him, his heart picked up speed.

The face was round, he saw, puffy and rounded as well as white. Like a face that's been underwater a long time, he thought. Drowned.

From a long way behind him, from where it was light and warm, Jim shouted, "Are you going to shut that door?"

Bill's answer was a dry little cough in his throat. "Ack. Ack."

Still the face hung there, glowering. And then it moved. Toward him. Drifting, floating, it bobbed nearer, as though blown by the wind or carried along by water. All the time it stared at him.

Bill's locked knees melted and sagged. With them wobbling beneath him, he turned and ran for the other end of the shop, for Jim and light and warmth. Looking back over his shoulder, he saw that the face was closer still, almost at the door. It was going to drift right through the doorway, into the shop. It was coming to get him!

As Bill neared the circle of yellowish light, Jim's head jerked up in surprise, and Jim's stare locked onto something behind him. So Jim could see it, too! It was real, and it was close behind him! Bill leaped the last few feet to Jim and hid behind him.

Jim said, "Evening, Officer. Anything we can do for you?"

Another voice said, "Just looked in to see why the light was on. What's up with the lad?"

"Dunno," Jim said. "We'm just rewinding these coils, fix this up for the morning. You want a cup of tea?"

Bill looked out from behind Jim to see a big policeman standing in front of the motor. A Warwickshire policeman, with a black badge on a black helmet and black buttons on a black coat. Nothing at all to catch the light.

"What's up?" the policeman said to Bill.

The only part of the policeman that caught the light had been his pale, pudgy face between the high, black collar of his uniform and his black helmet.

"I thought you was the gypsy girl!" Bill said.

"I am on me day's off," said the policeman. "But I don't bring me tambourine on duty."

My father used to tell this story when we were scared of ghosts. He used to say to us what Bill had said to him. "That's ghosts for you," Bill said.

The Mysterious Girl at the Pool

Juanita Havill

SUMMER DAYS are all alike. They melt into one another, and all you remember is going to the pool, doing chores, or sitting around reading. But one day last summer stands out crystal clear. I even remember the date: August 11.

I rode my bike to the pool. When I got there, I didn't see anyone I knew except some goofy boys from school. I wasn't about to play with them.

I plopped my towel down on the cement and went right to the deep water. I'm short for my age but swim better than most eleven-year-olds, so the lifeguards never hassle me about being in the deep.

I dived in. The cold water felt great. I swam laps to warm up, then found a popsicle stick by the ledge and decided to play chop-chop. It's a game I usually play with my friends. One of us dives in with the stick, takes it to the bottom, lets it go, and hurries back to the ledge to climb out. Whoever spots the stick screams "chop-chop" and goes for it. I'm pretty good. I can even find it when I'm the one who took it down. Then I get another turn. When I play alone, I take the stick down and see how fast I can find it.

I was staring at the water waiting for the stick to surface when I saw a girl I didn't recognize. She swam across the pool, then climbed out and sat on the ledge beside me. She wore a strange-looking orange bathing suit. It wasn't cut high on the leg like my suit. Instead, it hung down like shorts.

She held up my stick and said, "Can I play chop-chop with you?"

"Sure," I said.

She dived in with the stick. I strained to see where she went. She must have been able to hold her breath for a long time because she swam back to the ledge underwater. She climbed out and shouted, "Chop-chop," and had the stick before I even saw it.

Again and again she took the stick down and sighted it. She moved through the water like a dolphin. She was tiny and thin and had long brown hair and blue eyes. Her hair was so long I wondered why the guards didn't make her wear a cap. They didn't seem to notice.

Finally I won, but I couldn't help feeling that she had let me win.

"I'm hungry," I said, instead of taking the stick down. "Want to get a snack with me?"

"I'll come," she said, "but I'm not hungry."

Sitting on a bench outside the pool, I peeled the paper from my ice cream and offered her the first bite. She shook her head. "That's why you're so skinny," I said. I was curious to know who she was. "I'm Jackie Peterson. What's your name?"

"Roxanne Mainz," she said. "My folks have the flower shop downtown."

Maybe that's why I didn't know her. In our town we have two schools, kindergarten through eighth grade. Downtown goes to Edison School. I go to Jefferson.

"I haven't seen you here before. Don't you swim much?" I asked.

"I love to swim," she said, but her blue eyes darkened the way the sky does when clouds blow in front of the sun.

I shivered despite the hot afternoon. "Who's your teacher this year?"

"Mrs. Johns," she said. "I had Mrs. Wade last year."

I knew some of the teachers at Edison, but not either of them.

I finished my ice cream and threw the sticky wrapper in the garbage. "Do you like to dive off the board, Roxanne?"

Roxanne looked a little uneasy. She didn't answer.

"Let's go." I jumped up and ran toward the dressing

room. I could feel Roxanne following me without actually hearing her bare feet spank the cement walk. I was thinking about our chop-chop game. I'm pretty good at diving. This would be a chance to make up for my lousy chop-chop score.

I stood in line at the diving board in front of Roxanne. I could feel her watching me as I did a simple dive.

Roxanne didn't take her turn. "Go ahead," she said in a tone that kept me from coaxing her.

Next, I did a jackknife and almost touched my ankles.

"You're good" was all she said. When I climbed out, she motioned for me to go ahead again.

I decided to try a forward flip and go in feet first. I have to concentrate on flips because I have trouble getting enough oomph. I approached the end of the board and rose lightly into the air. I dived with my eyes closed tight.

Then I heard a loud noise. At the same time something clobbered me on the back of the head. It hurt so much I scrunched my shoulders. I knew I was sinking in the water, but I couldn't get my arms to move, and my legs felt heavy. I stared through the blue-green water, not even minding the sting of chlorine. I opened my mouth to cry out and choked on the rush of water. I was scared, more scared than I've ever been in my life.

Then Roxanne's face was right in front of mine. She grabbed my wrists and pulled me upward. I think

I must have closed my eyes because I didn't see her after that.

When I opened my eyes again, I saw the lifeguard. Two of those goofy boys were standing beside him. The lifeguard wouldn't let me talk or move. "Stay still," he told me. "Your mom is on her way. She's going to take you to the doctor."

I listened to his blurred words, trying to put together what had happened. I began to feel better and sat up. "Roxanne." I looked around. "Where's Roxanne?"

"Who?" The lifeguard was staring at me.

"Roxanne. The girl in the orange suit. We were swimming together."

One of the boys pointed to his head and made little circles with his index finger. "She's been swimming alone," he said. "And talking to herself the whole time."

"I thought you were playing some kind of game," the lifeguard said.

"Roxanne and I were playing." I was going to tell him where she went to school, but he put his hand on my shoulder.

"Calm down. You hit your head pretty hard on the board."

Mom took me to Dr. Shepard's. I was all right, but Mom said I couldn't go swimming for two days. She told me no more flips off the board for a while.

I told her about Roxanne. "The Mainzes?" she said. "I don't think they have a girl your age. They're a bit old. Maybe a granddaughter is visiting."

"Roxanne told me she went to Edison School. She had Mrs. Wade last year."

"Betsy Wade?" Mom shook her head. "She retired years ago."

The next day Mom took me downtown with her to run an errand. While she went to the drugstore, I walked up the street to Mainz Flower Shop. I wanted to thank Roxanne for saving me.

"Excuse me," I said to the woman behind the counter. "Are you Mrs. Mainz?"

"No, I'm her sister. I work here in August when Helen goes on vacation with her husband." The woman had curly white hair and a thin, wrinkled face. She looked old to be Roxanne's aunt.

Roxanne must have gone with them, I decided. That's why she left so quickly. She had to get ready for vacation. "Did they leave yesterday afternoon?"

"They left last week. They always leave well before the eleventh."

Something in the woman's voice made me uncomfortable, but I had to ask about Roxanne. "Didn't Roxanne go with them?"

"Roxanne?" The woman looked annoyed, as if she had to explain something all over again for the umpteenth time.

"Roxanne Mainz," I said. "I met her at the pool yesterday. She told me she lived here."

The woman stared at the bouquet of daisies on the counter. "Roxanne Mainz drowned thirty years ago," she said.

That didn't make sense. Why was she telling me about a Roxanne who had drowned thirty years ago? Roxanne had saved my life at the pool yesterday.

"She was an excellent swimmer," the woman said. "It was an accident. She slipped and hit her head on the diving board." The woman picked up the flowers and turned to go into the back room. She looked over her shoulder at me as if she'd just remembered I was there. "It's not the first time she's come back."

Suddenly I felt cold, as if I had dived into icy water. My whole body was one big goose bump. I bolted outside and ran down the street to the drugstore. The sight of my mom stepping onto the sidewalk made me feel safe and warm.

"Did you see Roxanne?" Mom asked.

"No, she doesn't live there," I said. Then I added, "Anymore."

The Airi

An Indian Ghost Story

Deepa Agarwal

ONLY A PALE glimmer of light remained when Bishan Singh began the long trek back to his village. He glanced at the sky and realized that even at his best speed, he could never hope to reach home before dark. In winter, night fell sudden and quick in the hills. And the sky had been overcast all day, so dusk had set in even earlier than usual.

"Spend the night in town," his friends had urged. They had come that morning to sell vegetables and other produce from their terraced fields. Although they had intended to return home early, they'd met up with a chatty man from another village, and as his anecdotes stretched on, the afternoon slipped away. So they decided to stop over for the night and return the next morning.

Ordinarily, the farmers didn't mind the long walk home. But on a snowy evening like this, it was a different matter. Not because of the cold. Fear of the *airi* kept them from the road tonight.

"You won't catch me going through the forest," Jeevan said with a nervous laugh. "And you shouldn't take the risk, either, Bishan. Didn't you hear what happened to Khim Singh?"

"Yes," Har Singh continued, his face full of a nameless fear. "It was just a year ago. He wouldn't listen, I heard. Insisted on walking home late on a snowy night. The next day they found him wandering in the forest, babbling nonsense. He was holding a pair of silver anklets in his hands, turning them round and round to make them jingle. He's never been right in the head since."

Bishan Singh shook his head. "That fellow was never quite right to begin with," he said. "Besides, my little daughter is sick. I must bring this medicine to her."

His companions exchanged glances. They looked scared—no, terrified. But Bishan Singh calmly picked up his bag and walked away.

As he trudged up the sloping path that led to his village, Bishan Singh was sorry he'd lingered in town. Not that he was afraid like the others. It was all nonsense, this talk of the airi, the female ghost who appeared when the ground was covered with snow. People said she looked just like a normal woman, only her airies, or heels, were where her toes should have been. She was supposed to possess men's minds, turn them inside out. But Bishan Singh was never one for believing such stuff.

All the same, he felt uneasy as he walked along. The sky was shadowy, and the tall trees loomed beside the road so silent, so still. Apart from the occasional slither and crash of a mass of snow sliding to the ground, he heard no sound but the *tramp, thud, tramp* of his feet ringing loud and lonesome in his ears. To cheer himself up, he began to hum a tune. Soon he warmed up into full-throated song. Bishan Singh was a good singer, much in demand at festivals and celebrations.

He sang song after song, hardly noticing the growing darkness around him. When he finally thought of switching on his old flashlight, its dim, yellow beam rested on a familiar landmark. He was almost halfway home!

"It's ridiculous," he said aloud, "that the others should have been afraid. Have we ever seen an airi in this forest?" He laughed so loud that the silent trees quivered with the sound.

Suddenly something made him go still—a jingle so distant and soft that for a moment he thought it might be an insect. But when he heard it again, it seemed to have a metallic sound. Perhaps it came from the village below the road. Sound traveled far at night in the cold, crisp air.

He began to hum as he tramped on. But then the

noise came again, louder this time. Curious, Bishan Singh turned and played the beam of his flashlight all around. But he saw nothing.

He stepped forward again, and the sound followed him. As he continued on, it grew louder and louder, filling his head, disturbing the rhythm of his steps . . . a silvery tinkle, like numerous little bells jingling together.

Bishan Singh stopped. It was the sound a woman's anklets make when she walks. But why would a woman be alone in the forest at this time of night? Maybe she had been gathering wood and hadn't noticed that it was getting late, or maybe she had lost her way. Should he wait?

As he stood there undecided, another thought crept into his head, making his scalp tingle. No! Bishan Singh thought. Such things don't exist. But when the tinkling sound came again, he felt his heart lurch sickeningly.

He began to walk as fast as he could. *Squish, squelch* went his feet on the slushy ground. His breath hung about him like puffs of smoke. The jingling seemed to recede as he hurried, hurried, hurried on.

Then he heard a huge CRASH!

It was so loud and sudden that he jumped, and a strangled cry escaped him. He looked around, panting, sweating in spite of the freezing cold. Then he burst into nervous laughter. It was only a deodar tree discharging its load of snow.

Shivering, he rushed on, despite his weariness. His

feet felt numb, wooden; his legs stiff and heavy. But he hurried because the *jingle, jingle, jingle* was creeping up on him again.

His heart thumped like a mighty drum. He barely noticed the pale sickly glow of the moon on the ground or the eerie light reflecting from the patches of snow on the hillside. The yellow beam of his flashlight wavered uncertainly on the ground ahead.

The sound was right behind him now! His chest grew tight; his breath stopped. He thought he could hear the swish of a woman's *ghaghra*.

Desperately he ran on, rigid like a puppet, not daring to look right or left or even straight up, just in case. The anklets rang in his ears, maddening, terrifying.

But it was no use.

"Why are you running away, Bishan Singh?" a woman's voice said.

From the corner of his eye, he glimpsed a tall shape in a voluminous black ghaghra. A film of ice crept up his back. How did she know his name?

"No, no, *didi*! I'm not running," he managed to reply, though his mouth was as dry as paper and his lips frozen stiff. "I must get home to my sick child."

"Didi! Didi! You called me an older sister!" He heard peal after peal of chilly laughter, and his knees knocked together in spite of his efforts to control them.

I'm done for, he thought. But somehow he found the courage to say, "Don't you have any brothers?" The words came out breathless, jerky.

"No, you're the only one, Bishania." She laughed again, a sound as piercing as hundreds of glass pieces flying at him. "So," he heard her say, "where are you coming from?"

"From the town, didi," he replied, trying to keep his teeth from chattering.

"From the town. Ahhh. No wonder you're in a hurry. Your wife must be waiting to see the presents you've brought."

"N-no. My child is ill. I have some medicine for her." This woman is not an airi, Bishan Singh thought desperately. An airi wouldn't waste time talking like this. He tried to remember all the stories he'd heard, but his thoughts were such a jumble that he couldn't recall a single one.

"So you bought nothing for your wife?" The woman sounded angry. Bishan Singh quaked as a vague memory surfaced. If she was an airi, she wouldn't cast a shadow. He forced himself to look down, but the faint light from the flashlight was no help, and the looming shadows of the trees obscured everything.

"Uh—yes, yes, I did," he forced himself to reply. "I bought some glass bangles and—and—a sari." If only he could keep her talking till he got to the village. It was not too far now. "Yes," he went on, "she wanted a sari. She doesn't want to wear a ghaghra. She wants to be modern like the town women—"

The woman laughed, and Bishan Singh jumped. The sound seemed to come from way above his head!

It couldn't be. The woman had appeared to be his height. He willed himself to look—a quick glance from the corner of his eye. He almost choked on his terror. She towered over him now!

"Why not? Why not?" he heard her say. "What else did you get?"

Somehow he managed to reply, "Sweets, shoes for my son, toys . . . medicine for my daughter . . ." An airi could grow as tall as the tallest pine tree, he'd heard.

"And nothing for your didi—hunh?"

"Of course I did! I bought a sari for you, too!" Would that placate her, save him?

"A sari!" she whooped with fearful joy. "Give it to me!"

"All right!" Bishan Singh's hands shook so badly as he fumbled in his bag that he thought he'd drop everything. Where was the sari he'd bought for his wife? At last he pulled it out.

A chilly hand touched his, and an awful cold numbed his bones. He shuddered as the beam of his flashlight slid down the length of the woman's ghaghra. When it reached her feet, he saw a pair of heels where her toes should have been.

His legs seemed to turn to stone, rooting him to the ground. He felt the sari being torn from his hand with such a force that it dragged him along with it. Suddenly he jerked out of his stupor, turned on his heels, and ran for dear life!

"Bishania . . . wait . . . Bishania . . . wait . . . *wai-ai-ait!*"

The words swooped into his ears, numbing him like venom. But Bishan Singh ran on, even though his legs felt as heavy as lead and his bag dragged him down as if it weighed a ton. Worse, the *jingle-jangle* seemed to have entered his ears permanently. It went on and on and on . . .

"What's the matter?" his wife cried, opening the door. "Is something chasing you? A leopard? A wolf?"

"Nothing, nothing! It's—it's the cold." He sank to the ground near the fire, hugging himself to stop the shivering. His wife bustled to get him a glass of hot, spicy ginger tea.

Bishan Singh's son was already going through bundles, pulling out the sweets, the toys, the medicine, the—

"Oh!" Bishan Singh heard his wife exclaim. "These must have cost a lot of money. They're beautiful!"

Bishan Singh turned around slowly. His wife held a pair of heavy silver anklets in her hand.

"But—," he began, then stopped. They looked old, and the little bells along the borders jingled faintly as his wife turned the anklets in her hand to show him.

Bishan Singh froze, then burst into crazy laughter. The *jingle, jingle, jingle* grew louder and louder in his ears, shutting out even the sound of his own heartbeat.

Some lucky impulse moved him to tear the anklets from his wife's hands and fling them into the fire. He and his family watched, terrified, as the anklets wriggled and slithered, hissing like venomous snakes till the fire turned them to shapeless lumps of metal. Gradually the jingling sound died away.

Bishan Singh shuddered, turned away, and sighed deeply. The wonderful silence told him that he was really safe now. He had destroyed the anklets—and escaped Khim Singh's terrible fate.

Bones

Frank O. Dodge

*T*IFFANY LANDRY SAT on the beach with her legs spread out and dug in the sand. Suddenly her tin shovel struck something hard. From under the sand a voice said, "Belay, there! That 'urt."

Tiffany jerked back, startled. She watched in amazement as the sand stirred and first one fleshless hand, then another, worked itself free and began scraping. As the sand fell away the frightened girl beheld a grinning skull. More ripples, and an apparition of white bones sat up. It gouged the sand from its eye sockets and looked at her. "'Oy," it said.

The girl scrambled to her feet and backed away, one hand to her mouth. "You're a skeleton!"

The skull tilted downward. The bones creaked a

little, and the joints popped slightly. The skeleton looked at Tiffany. "By thunder, I *am* a skeleton. I don't suppose ye know 'ow I got this way?"

Tiffany stared, torn between fright and curiosity. She shook her head. "You don't know?"

"Let me fink. Fings are hazy. Me nyme's George Murphy. Aye, George. Me shipmytes called me Long George—that's on account of I'm tall, ye see." He looked at Tiffany. "We took th' galleon *Santa Inez* off Dry Tortugas. Full o' gold, she were, from Panama. Then . . . a little brigantine . . . French, she were, out o' Hispaniola. That's where we got th' chest o' jewels."

Tiffany stared. "You're a pirate?"

Long George nodded. "Aye, girl. A pirate." He looked down at his bare bones. "Well, I guess I should say I *were* a pirate. I sailed along wiv Jolly Ned Teach o' Bristol aboard *Queen Anne's Revenge*."

"Jolly Ned Teach of Bristol? I've never heard of him."

"Mayhap ye've 'eard o' Blackbeard?"

"Oh! Yes, I've read about Blackbeard. He was a terrible man."

"Well, aye, Cap'n did 'ave a bit of a temper and a chancy sense o' 'umor. 'E once shot the first myte, Israel 'Ands, in th' knee just because 'e 'adn't shot nobody recently. Israel was a bit put out over that, 'e was, but 'e laughed right 'eartily at the joke to keep from gettin' shot through th' 'ead."

"Are you serious?"

"Oh, aye. Quite th' joker was Jolly Ned. . . ." Long

George scratched his head with fleshless fingers, making a grating sound that clawed at Tiffany's nerves.

She shuddered. "I wish you wouldn't do that."

"Oh, sorry. I just remembered somefing."

"What?"

"'Ow I got t' be a skeleton."

While Long George dredged his memory, Tiffany imagined the beach as it must have looked centuries earlier.

A big blood-red ship hove to and dropped anchor in the little cove. Sea gulls squawked and took flight at the splash and rumble of the anchor cable. Two dolphins made hastily for the open sea. The vast spread of canvas was furled expertly, and the ship rode to the slack tide. On her stern the gilt name *Queen Anne's Revenge* flashed in the sunlight.

A big man with a tricorn hat clamped over a red silk scarf eased the two baldrics that crisscrossed his chest, supporting six loaded pistols. He stroked his bushy raven beard and bellowed, "Lower away th' jolly boat."

Pulleys squealed and ropes creaked as deck hands swung the rowboat overboard. The wild-looking man watched as they lowered a small but heavy brass-bound chest into the boat.

Edward Teach, or "Blackbeard," was feared by all who ventured into the waters of the New World—even the other captains of the Brotherhood of the Coast. In addition to the six pistols slung across his chest, two more were thrust through the scarlet sash that circled his long blue box coat. A cutlass, a curved, cup-hilted sword, hung at his side. A pair of knee-length, wide-legged petticoat breeches, red-and-white striped stockings, and silver-buckled shoes completed his attire. Teach motioned for two of the hands to man the boat and then slid down the Jacob's ladder behind them. "Give way, rot yer eyes. Put yer backs t' them oars." The men heaved at the sweeps, and the little craft leaped shoreward across the sparkling water.

Long George jumped into the gentle surf and dragged the bow of the jolly boat onto the beach. Blackbeard stepped ashore. "Move smartly," he growled. "Rot yer blood, ye scum, move! We've not th' whole day. 'Tis less than an hour 'til th' turn o' th' tide. Would ye leave us high an' dry fer th' king's ships t' find?" The great black beard split in a roaring laugh. "Lieutenant Maynard'd give a year's pay t' find me aground! Stir yer stumps, ye swabs, an' look alive."

The sailors heaved the heavy chest out of the boat and carried it up the beach, their feet sinking in the sand. In a small glade a short distance into the thick forest, Teach took bearings from several landmarks. "Dig here."

A quarter-hour later Teach grunted, "Deep enough." The sailors dropped the chest into the hole and picked up shovels to bury it. Without warning Blackbeard drew two long pistols and fired. Bristol Jack fell dead atop the treasure chest, and Long

George, severely wounded, ran for the beach. He had just reached the jolly boat when Blackbeard's third bullet crashed into his back, plunging him facedown into the surf.

Teach returned to the glade and filled the hole containing the treasure and the body of Bristol Jack. He tamped the earth firmly over the grave and went back to the jolly boat. He kicked George's body aside, climbed into the boat, and rowed for the ship. In the gently washing surf Long George's corpse rolled limply, sand beginning to build up against its seaward side.

As Teach had warned, the tide began to ebb, leaving George high and dry. The tide turned. Waves washed over George, and more sand built up against him. By the next tide turn he was covered. Tides came and went. George sank gradually into the sand.

Tiffany took her hands from her mouth, her eyes big and round. "He really shot you in the back?"

Long George nodded, his neck bones creaking. "Shot me dead, 'e did."

The skeleton stood up and looked around. Nothing was as he remembered it. Gone was the thick forest. In its stead, a long sweep of lawn ran down the gentle slope from a big white house.

Petticoat breeches and a moldy leather belt still clung to George's bony pelvis. He hitched up his trousers and tightened the belt. He knelt and scrabbled through the sand until he disinterred a rusty cutlass, which he thrust through the belt. "There," he said.

"Feel bloody naked, I do, wivout a weepon." He tapped the hilt of the cutlass. "Wiv old Martha 'ere I feel some better. A pannikin o' grog an' I'd be a new man. . . ." The skeleton looked down at himself and chuckled. "Not much left o' th' old man, is there, girl? Say, wot's yer nyme, any'ow, sweet'eart?"

Tiffany dipped a little curtsy. "Miss Tiffany Landry, Master Murphy."

George seemed to grin. "Call me Long George, Mistress Tiffany. It 'pears we're shipmytes." He bowed clumsily. "An' a spritelier myte I never sailed wiv afore." He sat cross-legged and looked at the girl. "'Pears t' me I'm properly marooned." He waved a hand at the little cove. "Th' *Revenge*'s sailed . . . long ago. . . ." He started. "'*Ow* long ago, Mistress Tiffany?"

Tiffany shook her head. "I don't know."

"Wot year's this?"

"It's 2000."

George shook his head. "Nigh t' three 'undred years! Properly marooned indeed!" He looked forlorn. "Wot's t' become o' me, lass? Nothin' left but bones. Wot ship'd sign me on?"

Tiffany took the skeletal hand between her own soft palms. "I don't know, Long George, but I'm sure my daddy can think of something. Let's go ask him."

George shrugged, his bones rattling. He seemed to smile. "Don't ye think yer da might be summat confounded t' see me?"

Tiffany patted his hand. "You don't scare *me*."

George sighed. "Don't seem t' be much other choice, do there?" He rose to his feet, and the two walked hand in hand toward the big white house. They had left the sand and crossed several yards of neat grass when Long George suddenly stopped, as though he'd run into an invisible wall. He struggled to go forward, but something held him back.

Tiffany looked at him in surprise. "What's wrong?"

George stepped back. "'Tis as I feared. I'm bound t' this beach. 'Tis where I died." Disconsolate, he retraced his steps to the water's edge. He dropped to the sand and crossed his legs. "Mistress Tiffany, a beached sailor's a sorry fing." The skull turned toward the open sea. "Never t' feel th' 'eave of a deck under yer feet. Never t' 'ear th' singin' o' th' riggin'." His voice fell to a whisper. "Never t' lay aloft on a stormy night t' reef sails wiv th' wind screechin' in yer face . . . th' sea a welter o' waves 'igher than yer top-m'sts . . . th' ship plungin' 'er 'ead into them waves an' shakin' 'er shoulders t' struggle up t' dive into th' next one . . . a fing alive an' fightin' fer 'er life. Th' canvas in yer 'ands threatenin' t' pull ye from th' footropes an' throw ye into th' sea . . . ye're never more alive. . . ." He looked down at his bare bones and laughed grimly.

Tiffany sat entranced at George's words. She looked at the calm rollers entering the cove to break gently beside them and envisioned the wild and stormy scene the skeleton described. Goose bumps rose on her arms. "Oh, Long George! I'm so sorry. . . ."

George took her warm hand. "I fank ye, little mistress; yer understandin' takes some o' th' pain away."

Tiffany stood up. "I'm going to get Daddy."

*   *   *

Mr. Landry listened to his daughter's tale. "And this
. . . pirate . . . is waiting for me down on the beach?"

"Yes, Daddy. He really needs help."

"H'm. A skeleton, you say?"

A frown line appeared between the girl's brows.
"You're laughing at me."

"Well, honey, you have to admit . . ."

Tiffany tugged at her father's hand, pulling him
from his chair toward the window. "Look."

Mr. Landry looked, and his eyes opened wide.
There was someone sitting on the sand at the water's
edge, and either he was impossibly pale or it *was* sunlight glinting off bare bone. He swallowed.

"See, Daddy, I told you so."

Long George rose to his feet as Tiffany returned
with her father. He knuckled his forehead as if saluting
an officer. "G'day, yer worship. Mistress Tiffany said
ye might be kind enough t' aid an old sailor stranded
in such a pickle as none've ever 'eard of afore."

Mr. Landry cleared his throat. "That's for sure."
He sat abruptly. "I don't believe it! One of Blackbeard's men?"

"Aye." George hung his head. "Yer honor, I'll not
deny th' blood on me 'ands. Piratin's a bloody business, an' I'd not blame ye if ye refused yer 'elp. I'll not
bore ye wiv a long tale o' bitter persecution wot drove
me t' sail against all flags." The eyeless skull turned
toward Tiffany. "Mistress, ye're th' first 'uman wot's
spoke t' Long George wi' kindness, an' I'd not 'ave ye

fink ill o' me. If th' flesh were still on me back, ye'd see th' scars o' th' whip wot nearly flogged me t' death fer stealin' a few ounces o' bread t' feed me starvin' kiddie, wot died anyway when th' beak sentenced me t' transportation t' th' colonies as a slave fer th' Jamaican plantations. . . ." The skeleton waved a hand in dismissal. "Don't matter. . . ."

Tiffany's father cleared his throat and patted the bony shoulder. "I can surely see your need, but I don't have the slightest idea how I can be of help to a ghost."

George touched Mr. Landry's hand. "Ye've 'elped a'ready just by listenin', yer worship."

"Thanks, but that doesn't tell us what to do with a living dead man."

George chuckled. "I see yer point, yer honor. Ye could 'ardly 'ave me 'angin' about t' introduce t' yer friends." The skeleton paused. "But there's somethin' I can do fer ye. Come."

Mr. Landry and Tiffany followed as George walked toward the house. The skeleton stopped when he reached the invisible wall that held him prisoner. "I figger this must be th' farthermost I done come ashore. This 'as t' be th' spot where me an' poor Bristol Jack buried Blackbeard's treasure." The skeleton drew the cutlass from his belt and jabbed it into the ground. "Dig 'ere. Jack won't mind."

The three returned to the beach and sat in silence, pondering the situation. Suddenly Long George looked seaward. "Wot?"

Tiffany and her father followed George's pointing finger. A thick white fog was rolling swiftly into the cove. In a matter of seconds it enveloped them in an impenetrable blanket. They sat, stunned; then the fog vanished. Something had changed. Tiffany gave a little cry. "Look!"

Just outside the cove a big, blood-red ship with towering canvas heeled to the wind. From her aft gunports smoke billowed, followed by a dull boom of cannon fire. A second smaller, swifter ship appeared. Her bow-chasers, a pair of long nine-pounders, barked, and a cloud of splinters erupted from the red ship's taffrail and swept the quarterdeck. The helmsman collapsed. A huge black-bearded man heaved the corpse aside and took over the wheel.

Long George leaped to his feet and ripped off an excited oath. "It's Teach! *Queen Anne's Revenge!* She's back! An' there! That's Maynard's ship! 'E's been 'oundin' Blackbeard fer more'n a year an' now 'e's caught 'im!" The red ship's fore topmast fell and hung amid a tangle of rigging, making the vessel swing into the wind and lie dead in the water, listing heavily. The tilt rendered her guns useless, and Maynard pounded her unmercifully with his nine-pounders. The mizzenmast fell. Sections of her rail splintered, and holes appeared in her side. Maynard closed in and swept her decks with grapeshot, bags of leaden balls that spread in a murderous pattern. Grapnels were flung, and the two vessels warped together. Maynard's boarding party leaped, howling, over the rails, replacing the sound of cannon fire with the rattle of steel against steel and shouts of victory.

Tiffany and her father stared at Long George. But the skeleton was gone. In its place stood a muscular man in wide breeches with a long braided pigtail hanging down his whip-scarred back. George looked at the girl and knelt, taking her small hand to his lips. "God bless ye, Mistress, ye've gi'en me life! Yer pardon, Master Landry, but I want to be wiv Maynard when 'e tykes th' *Revenge*. I've a score t' settle wiv bloody Ned bloody Blackbeard Teach!" He ran to the jolly boat drawn up at the water's edge and tugged it into the surf. He heaved at the oars, pulling rapidly toward the embattled ships.

As the little rowboat distanced the shore, it began to waver and grow dim, as did the two tall ships. The nearer the jolly boat came to the ships, the dimmer they became and the fainter the sounds of battle. The air seemed to blink, and Tiffany and her father found themselves looking at an empty, silent sea.

"Well," Mr. Landry took his daughter's hand, "that seems to be that!"

Tiffany looked at her father. "Do you think he'll be all right?"

Mr. Landry squeezed her hand. "I don't know . . . but I have a funny feeling he will."

The two walked back toward the house. They stopped where George's cutlass marked the site of Blackbeard's treasure. Tiffany looked at her father. "Are we going to dig it up?"

"I don't think so. By the time the government takes its share and taxes the rest, there won't be enough left to justify disturbing poor old Bristol Jack."

"Thanks, Daddy." Tiffany reached for the rusty cutlass. "When I shine this up, it'll look real pretty over the fireplace."

Her father stopped her. "Leave it to mark the spot, sweetheart. Who knows? Maybe some night old George will come back for it . . . and his treasure."

Mary Jo
and the
Hairy Man

Eric A. Kimmel

ONE HOT afternoon in Round Rock, Texas, Mrs. Humphreys said to her daughter, "Mary Jo, I hear Granny Chittum is ailing. I've made her a basket of fried chicken, corn bread, and sweet potato pie. I'd like you to bring it over to her house for me."

"Yes, ma'am," said Mary Jo. She liked Granny Chittum a lot. Granny Chittum always had a story to tell about the old days in Round Rock. About the big cattle drives that used to come through the center of town. About Sam Bass, the outlaw, who was buried in the Round Rock cemetery. But most of all, Mary Jo liked to hear stories about spooks and haunts, like the time Granny Chittum met up with the Hairy Man on Brushy Creek Road.

"Do you think I might get to see the Hairy Man

someday?" Mary Jo asked her mother as she saddled up her horse, Eileen.

"Goodness gracious!" Mrs. Humphreys exclaimed. "I don't want you going anywhere near Brushy Creek Road after dark. Do you hear me, Mary Jo? Besides, there's no such thing as the Hairy Man."

"If there's no such thing as the Hairy Man, why can't I go by Brushy Creek whenever I like?"

"Never you mind," said Mrs. Humphreys, handing Mary Jo the basket. "Don't stay too long. I want you home by nightfall."

"Yes, ma'am," said Mary Jo. "Giddup, Eileen!"

Eileen stepped out at a slow walk. But after she crossed the ridge, out of sight of the house, she broke into a gallop, and off they went! Eileen was bony and cantankerous, but she could go like the wind when she'd a mind to.

It took Mary Jo less than an hour to get to Granny Chittum's house. She found Granny Chittum sitting on the porch in her rocking chair, smoking her pipe with her shotgun across her knees. As Mary Jo rode up, she blasted away at a couple of jack rabbits that were getting too close to her garden.

"Why, Mary Jo! What brings you here?"

"We heard you were sick. Mama sent over some fried chicken and corn bread. She made her own special sweet potato pie, too," Mary Jo said as she handed down the basket.

"I was sick, but I feel much better now," said Granny Chittum. "Please thank your mama for me.

And thank you, too, Mary Jo. You're very kind to go through such trouble."

"No trouble at all, ma'am," Mary Jo said.

Granny Chittum opened the basket. "I haven't seen fried chicken like this since the night my mother cooked dinner for Sam Bass!"

"You never told me that story."

"Then I'll tell it now."

By the time Granny Chittum finished telling how Sam Bass had washed and dried the dishes and ducked out the back door, still wearing her mother's apron, just as the Texas Rangers came riding up the road, daylight was starting to fade.

"I'd better get on home," said Mary Jo. "I promised I'd be back before dark."

"Don't go down Brushy Creek Road. I don't want the Hairy Man to get you," Granny Chittum said.

Mary Jo laughed. "Mama says there's no such thing as the Hairy Man."

"I know better," said Granny Chittum. "I've seen him."

Mary Jo and Eileen started for home. Soon they came to a fork in the road. The left fork went by Preacher Gibbons's place and the new church. The right led down to Brushy Creek.

"What do you say, Eileen? Left or right?"

Eileen snorted, shook her head, and turned right.

Not many people go down Brushy Creek Road even in the daytime. The live oaks growing on either side of the path intertwine their branches to form a thick canopy overhead. Mary Jo could hardly see the full moon. Riding between those trees was like going down a winding tunnel.

Mary Jo began to feel uneasy. Her skin prickled. She felt a knot in the middle of her belly. Maybe it wasn't such a good idea to go this way after all. On the other hand, Eileen ambled along with no more concern than if she were crossing the corral back home. Eileen had a nose for danger. If anything was lurking behind those trees, she'd be gone.

That made Mary Jo feel better. Mama's right, she thought. There's nothing down here 'cept some spooky old trees. Her skin stopped prickling, and the knot behind her belt buckle untied itself. She began singing softly to her horse.

> *Eileen, good night.*
> *Eileen, good night.*
> *Good night, Eileen. Good night, Eileen.*
> *I'll see you in my—*

Suddenly Eileen stopped in her tracks. Her ears went back, and her tail began swishing. It was still plenty dark, but moonlight shining through a break in the canopy made it just bright enough for Mary Jo to see what was standing up ahead.

It was as big as a barn and covered with long, wiry hair like a sheepdog. Two long, straight horns sprouted from its forehead. Its yellow eyes glowed like the lights on a midnight train. It had cougar's claws, cottonmouth fangs, and a knob on its tail that rattled and buzzed like a rattlesnake.

"Howdy, Mary Jo," the thing said in a voice that screeched like a rusty hinge.

No one needed to tell Mary Jo who was talking to her. "Howdy, Hairy Man," she answered.

"You wanted to see me. Well it looks like you got your wish."

"I reckon I did, Hairy Man."

The Hairy Man laughed long and hard. "Mary Jo, do you see these long, sharp horns of mine? I can spear you through and through."

"I see 'em, Hairy Man. I know that you can do that, too."

"Are you scared?"

"No, Hairy Man. I ain't scared." The truth was, Mary Jo was scareder than she'd ever been in her life, but she wasn't about to let on.

The Hairy Man bared his fangs. He spread his claws. "Mary Jo, do you see these claws of mine? I could tear you apart with one swipe. And these fangs, sharp as needles and dripping poison? One drop gets on your skin and you're dead!"

"I see 'em, Hairy Man. I believe you can do whatever you say."

"Are you scared now?"

"No, Hairy Man."

The Hairy Man grumbled. He lifted his tail and cracked it like a bullwhip. "Do you see this tail of mine, Mary Jo? You hear how it buzzes and rattles, like a pit full of rattlesnakes?"

"I see it and I hear it, Hairy Man. It's a frightful sound."

"Well, are you scared?"

"No, Hairy Man. I'm sorry. I'd be lying if I said I was."

The Hairy Man snarled at Mary Jo. "What's wrong with you, girl? You're supposed to be scared. I've been haunting Brushy Creek Road for five hundred years. I was here before the Mexicans, before the Spanish, even before the Indians! They've all been scared of the Hairy Man. One time I even scared Sam Bass. Now, don't tell me you're braver than him."

"No, I'm not, Hairy Man."

"Then why ain't you scared?"

"Well, you see, it's like this," Mary Jo began. "You may be big and hairy all over. You may have long horns. You may have sharp claws and cottonmouth fangs that drip poison. You may have a knob on your tail that rattles and buzzes like a pit full of rattlesnakes. That's all well and good. But, Hairy Man, I need to tell you I got something you ain't got, and that makes all the difference."

"What's that?" the Hairy Man growled.

"Eileen!"

Mary Jo gave her horse a kick and let loose the reins. Eileen leaped over the Hairy Man like a jack rabbit clearing a gully. She hit the ground running and never looked back.

Mary Jo leaned forward in the saddle and held tight to Eileen's mane as she tore down Brushy Creek Road at full gallop. But if Mary Jo thought she could outrun the Hairy Man, she was wrong. She glanced back and there he was—bounding along like a jack rabbit, two lengths behind and gaining!

"You can't outrun me, Mary Jo! I'm coming to get you!"

"Go, Eileen!" Mary Jo whipped her horse with the reins. Eileen put on an extra burst of speed. But the Hairy Man matched it. Soon he was only a length and a half behind.

Mary Jo had one chance left. If she could get across Brushy Creek, she'd be safe. Granny Chittum had told her that spooks and haunts can't cross running water. It was summer, and there wasn't much water running in Brushy Creek, but Mary Jo hoped it would do.

They were nearing the ford. Mary Jo saw a break in the trees. She heard water splashing over rocks. The Hairy Man came up right behind her. He reached out with his claws. . . .

Eileen jumped! She leaped from the bank and flew over the water like a horse with wings. She landed on the round rock in the middle of the creek and leaped again. Her shoes struck sparks from the stone.

"You won't get away from me!" the Hairy Man roared. He reached out for Mary Jo with those long, long arms. His claws scraped the rock like a piece of chalk screeching across a blackboard. But all he got was a hank of hair from Eileen's tail. The rest of her, with Mary Jo safe on her back, went galloping on home.

*　　*　　*

In the morning the sheriff rode down to the ford to investigate. He found an old hobo camped in the bushes. The sheriff questioned him, but the fellow'd been drunk the night before. Hadn't heard or seen a thing. Even so, everyone in Round Rock breathed a sigh of relief. "It was just a poor tramp," they all said. "There's no such thing as a Hairy Man!"

Mary Jo knew better. So did Eileen, but she wasn't talking.

Now, if you still have doubts after hearing this story, just wade into the middle of Brushy Creek some summer afternoon when the water's low. Take a look at the round rock. On top you'll see four circular marks shaped like horseshoes. Below are eight deep grooves that look as if they've been cut with a chisel—or two sets of long, sharp claws. And on your way home, make sure to stop and take a look at the street sign.

Why do you think they call it Hairy Man Road?

A Ghostly Game of Puckeen

An Irish Ghost Story

Kathleen M. Muldoon

ONCE UPON a bleak Irish morning, a spindly lad named Jack bade his mother good-bye and set out to seek his destiny. The salty sea mists drenched Jack's flimsy coat as he strode along. By nightfall, he could go no farther. He stopped at a farmhouse that nestled in the shadow of a dark castle. An old man ushered Jack inside and led him to a bench in front of an ample fire.

"What is it you're wanting, lad?" asked the farmer.

"Please, sir," said Jack, stifling a yawn. "I will gladly work your fields in the morning for supper and a warm bed tonight."

The farmer rubbed his hands together and paced before the mantel.

"Did you see that castle yonder?"

Jack nodded, one eye open, the other halfway to dreamland.

"I will put you in that castle in front of a fire three times the size of mine. There will be a table with every manner of meat and fish, and a bed as soft as moon cheese. I will lock you in, alone. In the morning, if you are still alive, I will give you a farmhouse and my daughter's hand in marriage, should you fancy her."

Jack bolted upright, sleepiness fleeing like a fox from the hunt. "I'll do it, if you send no one to kill me!"

"Not I," the farmer muttered. "'Twas my father's castle. Since his death, no man has spent the night and lived to face the morning. Four have tried."

"Sir, I have nothing of this world except courage," Jack replied.

True to the farmer's word, Jack soon found himself locked in a large room of the dismal castle. It was lit only by a roaring fire and two candles adorning a heavily laden table.

After feasting on roasted lamb, bread, and cheese, Jack stretched out on the floor before the hearth, intent on sleeping away the night and claiming his fortune in the morning. Before long, however, such a ruckus arose on the ceiling above his head that Jack jumped up, and an icy shiver pulsed down his back.

"I'm falling, falling," Jack heard a voice call. As he looked up, two legs, then a man's body, shoulder, arms, and head oozed through a hole in the ceiling.

The parts reassembled themselves into a white-headed figure in a triangular-shaped hat and waistcoat such as Jack's grandfather wore. Before Jack could shout or gasp, another spirit of a man appeared and then a third, each apparition more ancient than the one before.

Then, just as Jack thought he could bear no more, the first spirit took a puckeen from his waistcoat and began a furious game with the others, the second and third spirits against the first.

"I say," Jack squeaked, amazed he had a voice at all. "I say, that's hardly fair, two against one."

Without waiting for a reply, Jack joined the first ghost. They played all night, never exchanging a word, never pausing for rest. As the first sliver of sunrise seeped through the castle windows, Jack slumped onto a chair.

"Rest," he croaked. "Rest."

The three spirits stopped their frantic kicking and running and surrounded Jack. The first placed his hand on Jack's shoulder.

"We haven't rested for many years," he said. "Perhaps we can now that we've found someone with courage. The others all died of fright before they could help us.

"I was the farmer's father," he continued. He pointed to the other two spirits. "That was my father, and the eldest my grandfather. None of us has peace because in life we cheated many people. We cannot rest until our wrongs are righted."

Jack shrugged. "What can I do?"

"A white mare waits at the post," said the spirit. "Her saddlebags are filled with gold and a list of families deserving of our restitution. Ride the countryside until the gold is distributed. When you return, look toward the highest turret of the castle to see the results of your deed."

As the spirit stopped talking, the castle door opened, and in walked the farmer and his beautiful daughter.

"You . . . you're alive!" the farmer gasped.

Jack whirled around in his chair. The spirits were gone. Before he even touched the hand of the farmer's daughter, Jack jumped up, ran outside, and leaped onto the mare.

"I'll be back!" he shouted.

Jack rode uphill and down, over creeks and rivers, over fences and walls. He delivered the spirits' gifts to the shabbiest cottages in the villages. When at last the saddlebags were empty, Jack took the shortest route back to the castle. He tied the mare to the post, then looked up at the tallest turret just in time to see three snow-white doves soar to the heavens.

The castle door opened, and the farmer's enchanting daughter took Jack's hand and pulled him inside.

"Welcome home," she said.

The farmer insisted Jack and his new bride live in the castle beside his farmhouse. There they dwelt happily for the rest of their lives. The spirits had left the puckeen behind, and Jack put the ball on the mantel to remind him of the value of courage and honesty. And sometimes, on a winter's night, he told his children the story of how he and three spirits once played a ghostly game of puckeen.

Triple Anchovies

Marion Dane Bauer

"*I* WANT TO ORDER a pizza," I said into the telephone, letting my voice quaver a little so I would sound like an old lady. "The biggest you've got."

Kim was across from me, one hand over her mouth, practically choking on giggles.

"Yeah . . . the extra large," I agreed. "That'll be fine." I gave Kim a dirty look. If she started me giggling, too, the guy taking the order was sure to get suspicious. After all, I don't suppose we were the first kids on earth to think of ordering a pizza and having it sent to somebody else, someone who wouldn't expect it. We may have been the first to think of doing it on Halloween, though, and having it sent to Miss Dawson, the most ancient old lady in town, if not the universe. Why, she was so old she had probably been born before pizzas were invented!

"And I want green peppers on it," I said, "and onions and mushrooms. Lots of mushrooms."

Kim made a face. She *hated* mushrooms, but then she knew I hated green peppers and onions, for that matter. "Anchovies, Heather," she whispered. "Anchovies, too!"

I turned so I couldn't see Kim's face—I didn't want to take a chance of her making me laugh out loud—and added, my voice even more wavery than before, "And don't forget the anchovies, young man. I want triple anchovies."

Behind me I could hear Kim fall out of her chair and roll on the floor, snorting and choking. I suppose it was the "young man" that got to her . . . or the very mention of those dark, salty little blobs of fish neither one of us could abide. But of course, we weren't the ones who were going to have to eat *this* concoction.

It wasn't that we had anything against Miss Dawson, you understand. It was just that our mothers had decided we were too old for trick-or-treating this year, though how you can be the right age for something one time and "too old" just twelve months later is beyond me. So we had been at my house handing out candy all evening, some of it to kids our own age or even older. And I guess we were feeling pretty mean.

Anyway, Miss Dawson came to mind because she

lives on the corner of my block and because . . . well, not for any particular reason, really. We just needed to do something. Nothing that would hurt anyone, you understand, or get us into trouble, either. And I suppose we figured Miss Dawson was so old she wouldn't even realize someone was playing a trick on her. She would probably think it was meals on wheels, a bit late in the day. Or a friendly gift from her neighbors. Which it was . . . kind of.

I hung up the phone and turned to Kim, who was lying limply on the floor hiccuping giggles. "The next step in Operation Pizza," I told her, "is to set up a watch at Miss Dawson's house. We want to be there when she gets her first whiff of piping hot anchovies!"

The bare lilac bushes along the edge of Miss Dawson's yard didn't hide much, but we crouched behind them anyway. The last trick-or-treaters trailing by on the street didn't bother to turn into Miss Dawson's walk. She had her porch light on, as though she might be expecting them, but most of the parents had probably told their kids not to bother her.

A cold wind clattered the branches of the trees and passed between my ribs as well. Kim was scrunched down as close beside me as she could get, her teeth rattling like skeleton bones.

"I wish they'd hurry," she said, and I wished it, too. Actually, we'd only been there about five minutes, but I was already remembering how warm my house had been. It hadn't been so bad, really, sitting in front of the fire my dad had set in the fireplace, drinking hot cider, and answering the door now and then.

Miss Dawson passed in front of her living room window and stopped to look out. Her upper back was so bent that she reminded me of a turtle peering from its shell. I held my breath, though I'm sure she couldn't have seen us anyway. It was strange, squatting there in the dark while she seemed to be looking straight at us. I couldn't breathe properly until she moved away from the window again.

I was just about to ask Kim if she thought the guy taking our order might have figured it for a joke when a voice came from about two feet behind us. "What're you doing here?" it asked, real quietlike.

Kim's only answer was to topple over onto her nose with a little "Eeeep!" She's never been exactly what you could call poised. I practically jumped out of my skin, but I managed to scramble to my feet and turn around.

The boy must have been about our age, but it was obvious his mother hadn't told him he was "too old" for trick-or-treating. He was wearing the fanciest costume I'd ever seen. I mean, he looked like something out of an old-fashioned book, knickers and high-button shoes and a billed cap. Not a baseball cap, but one of those soft ones with a wide, stubby brim like you see on old men sometimes. He wasn't wearing a mask and he didn't have his face painted or anything like that, but it was all too strange to be anything but a costume.

"What're you doing at my house?" he repeated, more loudly this time. He acted very stern, but I could have sworn he was holding back a laugh.

"Your hou . . . house?" I stammered. "Nobody lives here except old Miss Dawson. Nobody has lived here but her for just about forever."

The boy didn't answer that. He just stood there, looking us up and down. You would think he'd never seen a couple of girls dressed in sweatshirts and jeans. Kim had gathered her wits enough to pick herself up off the ground by then.

"What's your name?" she asked, or squeaked, really.

"Prew," the kid said.

"Drew?" I repeated, but the boy shook his head.

"Prew," he corrected.

"Mine's Heather," I told him. "And this is Kim."

He smiled, not a welcoming smile exactly but like he thought our names were funny. Though I couldn't figure why someone named Prew would think anybody else's name was funny.

"You through trick-or-treating?" I asked.

"Trick-or-treating?" he repeated, like he'd never heard of such a thing. And then, before I could decide whether he was joking or just dumb, he asked, "You want to help with a Halloween prank?" He adjusted his cap, pulling it down onto his forehead at a cocky angle, his eyes shining with mischief.

"Uh . . . I guess so. Yeah. Sure," I answered, though I wasn't feeling sure about anything. What else were we about if not a prank, though I wouldn't have used such a funny, old-fashioned word to describe it. Still, whatever this boy had in mind would probably be better than having to explain what we were doing at "his" house . . . or about the pizza truck that was sure to show up any minute. He was probably a visiting relative, a distant grandnephew or something, and if he told Miss Dawson about our pizza "prank," she'd tell our parents for sure.

"What do you want to do?" Kim asked.

"How about hauling a buggy up on top of the school?" Prew came back with.

"A buggy?" Kim and I echoed. Was this strange kid talking about a baby buggy? And where were we supposed to find one of those? I didn't even know anybody who had one.

"Or we could go out to one of the farmers' fields and tip over corn shocks," Prew continued, clapping his hands like he was applauding his own idea. "Or better yet, outhouses right here in town."

Outhouses! I had heard of those. They used to sit in people's backyards and they were used for . . . Oh, yuck!

"Last year some of the bigger boys tipped over old Mr. Standberg's two-holer . . . with him in it! He thought if he sat up in it all night, no one would dare try. Was he *upset!*" And he laughed, though whether at the thought of the old man tipped over with the out-house or at his own pun was hard to tell.

Kim moved in closer to me, and I knew what she was thinking. This kid was a real nut case!

"Of course," Prew added thoughtfully, "if you're going to tip an outhouse, you do have to be careful not to fall in yourself."

"Ew!" Kim exclaimed, and she turned away, holding her nose.

"Nobody around here—," I started to say, but he wasn't listening.

"I know!" he cried. "I've got a better idea yet!" And he turned and started down the street, motioning us to follow.

I looked at Kim, who looked at me. Then we both shrugged and went after him. I must admit, though, I was hoping this new idea would be an improvement over tipping outhouses. Even nonexistent ones!

"We're going to miss the delivery," Kim hissed in my ear. I shrugged. If you want to know the truth, the whole pizza idea did seem pretty dumb by this time anyway. And a gust of sharp wind told me it was better to be moving than hanging around in somebody's bare bushes.

So we trotted along after Prew as though it was what we always did on Halloween, follow a boy we'd never met before through the night streets. The leaves crunched underfoot, crisp and dusty, and there was a smell of sweet wood smoke in the air, probably coming from my own house. Only we weren't going toward my house.

"Where are we going?" Kim whispered. She always asks me questions as though I'm supposed to know all the answers.

Before I could tell her that I didn't have the faintest idea, Prew stopped in front of the Methodist church. It's the oldest church in town, stone with a square bell tower that holds a real bell. Behind it and to one side, there's a cemetery. With real ghosts, I suppose. If you believe in such things.

I'd always figured that ghosts appear only to people who believe in them, which left me out for sure. My parents are both scientists, the kind of "rational thinkers" who answer every question with more facts than anybody wants to hear. When I was a little kid, they even told me the "facts" about Santa Claus, which I thought, even at the time, was a crummy thing to do.

"What are we going to do here?" I asked, not even trying to keep the sarcasm out of my voice. "Swing a dead cat over our heads to cure warts?"

Kim giggled, her nervous giggle, which isn't much different from her silly one or her downright scared one or her nothing-else-to-do-anyway one, unless you know her real well. Prew didn't even glance in our direction. Instead he started along the front walk of the church and turned abruptly into the cemetery.

Kim and I followed. "What better place to spend Halloween?" I murmured.

"I don't think the residents give out very good treats, though," Kim answered back. I could tell she was trying to sound totally cool. There was only a small slice of moon, so as we moved away from the streetlights, darkness settled around us like a vampire's cloak.

Kim kept in step with me, practically glued to my side.

Prew stepped up onto the edge of a tombstone near the side of the church and took hold of a low tree limb. "What we're going to do," he explained as he pulled himself up into the gnarled oak, "is give this town reason to believe in ghosts."

For an instant his white shirt and the white knee-stockings below his knickers stood out clearly, bright in the faint moonlight. Then, for just another instant, or perhaps only a fragment of one, I could have sworn the light passed right through him. It was like he was made of glass, or something even less substantial than glass. And then he disappeared behind a screen of dead leaves.

"Let's get out of here!" Kim moaned, but I stayed put.

"He's in the tree," I told her. "And we can go anyplace he can." Before she could answer, I stepped up onto the edge of the tombstone, took hold of the limb, and pulled myself up.

Kim scrambled after me. She's anything but a rational thinker, and I'm sure she wasn't about to be left alone among the gravestones, even a couple of dozen steps from the street. Anyway, we hadn't gone farther than the next branch before we saw Prew again, just as substantial as before.

"We're going to toll the bell," he explained as he

crawled out onto a thick branch overhanging the roof of the church.

"The way they do when someone dies?" Kim gasped.

"Are you crazy?" I demanded, still following. I'm no coward, but it doesn't take a whole lot of brains to figure out that if you ring a big loud church bell when it's not supposed to be ringing, someone will come to investigate. "We'll get caught for sure. Besides, ringing the bell won't make people believe in ghosts. They'll know it's kids."

Prew dropped off onto the flat roof. "We won't get caught because we aren't going to be anywhere near when it's ringing. In fact, no one is, except for our friends here." And he swept a hand in the direction of the dark cemetery. "So folks will just have to blame them. Don't you see?"

I didn't see. I didn't see anything at all, but I decided, reluctantly, that I would give him a chance to show us. Which he proceeded to do.

There were some louvers broken across one window, so Prew climbed through into the musty darkness of the bell tower. We followed. Dozens of pigeons and squirrels had been there before us, and the stone steps were cluttered and slippery. The cemetery below seemed positively friendly in comparison!

Prew moved on ahead to the small room where the monstrous bell hung. Then, groping in the near dark, he located the two bell ropes, each falling through a hole in the platform to the distant floor below. A fat one attached to a big wheel was for pealing the bell, and a much thinner one attached to an L-shaped piece of metal was for tolling.

Prew pulled the thin rope up until he had hold of the end, which he then handed to me. "Now, we'll take this out and tie it to a branch in the tree, one that moves nicely in the wind." His teeth gleamed when he grinned.

He was right to grin, too, because his idea worked! We tied the rope to a swaying branch, and before we could shinny down the tree and scurry out of the cemetery, the bell had let out three solemn *bongs* and a couple of *tinks*. The tinks were, I suppose, from times when the wind hadn't moved the branch far enough to pull the clapper the whole way. When it really connected, though, it was enough to make the hair on the back of your neck stand up and salute.

By the time we stopped again in the shelter of Miss Dawson's lilacs, I was feeling downright friendly toward this new kid. In fact, I was feeling so friendly I decided to let him in on the little trick we were playing on his great-aunt. I knew we had missed the fun of seeing her greet the delivery, but still the whole thing was kind of funny to think about.

"Anchovies?" he asked when I had finished explaining about the pizza. "What are they?"

"Fish," Kim told him.

"Little salty, stinky fish," I added. "They make anything they're on taste dreadful."

Prew smiled, a long, slow smile. "A great prank,"

he said, nodding, but then he glanced toward the house and added, almost sadly, "I guess it's time for me to go in . . . before I'm missed." In the distance, the bell bonged again, an exclamation mark for his words.

"When you get in, why don't you ask Miss Dawson for a piece of anchovy pizza?" Kim giggled.

"Does she know you're out?" I asked, just for something to say. The truth was, I didn't want him to go in.

The bell tolled loudly again.

"More or less," Prew said, looking back in the direction of the church. "Anyway, she probably figured it out the first time she heard that." He started toward the house.

I had thought he would go up to the front door, but instead he headed for the side of the house where a rickety rose trellis stretched up toward a second-story window.

Kim called to him in a worried voice, "You're not going to climb that old thing, are you?"

"It's the way I always come out." As Prew spoke he swung up onto the trellis and began to climb. Kim and I hurried to stand below him, though I don't suppose we would have done him much good if he had fallen. From the church, the bell continued to toll, not quite steadily but in a voice that couldn't be missed. I could hear people, up and down the street, opening their front doors and calling to one another in questioning voices.

The trellis must have been stronger than it looked,

because it didn't even tremble as Prew climbed. When he got to the top, he looked down and waved at us. And then he did something amazing. He pulled off his hat and waved with that, letting a mass of dark curls tumble down his back.

"Prew," I found myself saying. "Pru. Prudence." Miss Dawson's name was Prudence. I'd seen it on her mailbox every day of my life, though no one in the town ever used her first name as far as I knew. But what could it mean, this strange girl, named after the old woman, climbing in and out of an upstairs window in her house?

Kim clamped one cold hand on my wrist. "Look! The window! She can't . . ."

I looked. Pru was standing on the very top of the trellis, leaning toward the tightly closed window. There was no way she was going to be able to open it from the outside. The wind gusted, the church bell tolled mournfully, and Pru balanced there, high above the ground.

"Be careful," I called. But the bell, sounding again, drowned out my voice.

It was obvious, though, that Pru didn't need any kind of warning from me. She motioned, as if to tell us to watch, and stepped through the closed window. She simply moved through it, the way a shadow passes through glass, and then she was swallowed up inside the old house.

Kim and I stood rooted there, side by side, mouths gaping, staring at the blank window. After a moment,

we turned to one another, but neither could think of anything to say. Finally, by some unspoken agreement, we started across Miss Dawson's yard, heading for my house. As we passed the front porch, though, the door opened, and the old woman herself appeared on the porch.

"Hello, girls!" she called. "You must have come for a treat. Come in. Come in. I thought no one was going to stop at my house this year."

Kim and I stopped walking as suddenly as if our feet had been caught in a trap. Then, not knowing what else to do, we turned and climbed the steps to the porch.

"You're in luck," Miss Dawson was saying. "Somebody sent me a special Halloween treat."

"A treat?" I managed to stammer.

"Oh," she continued in a confiding way, "it was meant as a prank, I know, but I paid for it so the shop wouldn't suffer. I couldn't possibly eat it all myself, though. I was just hoping some nice youngsters would come by to share it with me."

Down the street, the church bell bonged.

"Someone must have died," Kim said without even a trace of a giggle, but Prudence Dawson only shook her head.

"More Halloween pranks, I think. In fact, I remember a time when I was a little girl . . ."

Her voice trailed off, but she reached up to set an imaginary cap at a jaunty angle, her eyes gleaming with mischief. She held the door wide for us. Just behind her on an antique hall table sat an enormous, flat box.

Already I could detect the aroma of anchovies.

The Glashtyn

A Ghost Story from the Isle of Man

Josepha Sherman

ONCE THERE LIVED a fisherman and his daughter, Nance. And a pretty young thing was she, with long, curly brown hair and eyes as blue as the sea. Nance kept their house and tended their little garden and the few chickens when her father was off at sea, and father and daughter were as happy as two people could be.

Only one thing secretly grieved the fisherman, and that was the memory of his dear wife, who'd died when their daughter was a baby. And with that memory was the worry of leaving Nance alone when he went out to sea.

But he must sail or there'd be no fish to catch and sell, so he said to his daughter, as he did every time he went off in his boat, "Now, you're to be wary while I'm gone and open the door to no stranger, be he man or . . . Other."

Nance laughed away his fears. "Have I not grown up in this place? And don't I know not to invite into this house any stranger, man or Other?"

So off the fisherman sailed in his small, swift boat, promising to be back before the sun had set. And his daughter gathered the eggs from their few chickens, spun a little wool, tended the garden, then brewed herself some nice, hot tea and sat peacefully, listening to the seabirds squealing high overhead.

But as the day moved toward night, great storm clouds came boiling up out of the west, and the girl stood up in alarm as thunder boomed and rain came torrenting down. Where was her father? Was he caught in the storm? Surely he would sail farther out, out of the wind and rain into calmer seas and wait. Just in case, she lit a lantern and placed it in their cottage's one window so that he would see the light if he was trying to get home, and not be lost. As the storm winds screamed about the cottage, Nance tried and tried not to worry.

A faint knock on the door woke her. "Dad?"

Was he hurt? Too weak to open the door himself? "Dad!"

Hastily, Nance flung open the door—

But this wasn't her father! This was the finest young man she had ever seen, with long hair like an inky black mane and great brown eyes set in a narrow face, dark as the skin of the Gypsies she'd seen once. But he wore fisherman's clothes and he was soaked to the skin.

"Was there a wreck?" Nance asked in fright. "Are you hurt?"

He shook his head.

"What is this? Can't you speak our tongue?"

He gestured only that he was tired and wished to rest. Nance remembered her father's warning about not opening the door to strangers. But all the fisherfolk knew that you must give help to anyone from a shipwreck, so she let the poor man in. He curled up in front of the fire and slept and he was still the most handsome man Nance had ever seen. But there was something so odd and foreign about him. . . .

All at once I wish the rooster were crowing in the dawn, she thought. For nothing Otherly, nothing of strange magic, could stand the touch of daylight.

Not sure of herself, hardly daring to breathe, Nance very, very gently brushed the stranger's long, dark mane of hair away from his face.

And she nearly screamed in shock. For his ears were not the rounded ears of a man but the sharply pointed ones of a horse. He was no man at all! This was a Glashtyn, a water horse who had taken on human shape. The Glashtyn enchanted humans, lured them into the sea—and drowned them!

Just then, the Glashtyn woke and smiled at her. If she had not seen those pointed ears, Nance would surely have thought it a mortal man's smile. He pulled

a string of lovely pearls from a pocket and laid it across her knee with a pleading look.

"You want me to come with you?" Nance brushed the pearls from her knee. "Oh no, I'll not take your gifts and I'll not come with you!"

With a shout of rage like a stallion's scream, the Glashtyn sprang to his feet. Catching her by the arm, he dragged her from the cottage. And his form began to change, from man to great black stallion, mane and tail whipping wildly in the wind.

"I'll not go with you!" Nance cried.

She screamed with all her might—and as she'd hoped, the rooster woke in surprise and began to crow. The great black stallion froze, flattening his ears against his head, sure that the dawn had come. With a snort of rage, he whirled and plunged into the sea.

Nance raced back to the cottage and bolted the door, waiting with heart pounding until at last the storm ended. It was truly morning now—and here came her father. Nance ran to him and flung her arms about his neck as though she would never let him go.

The Glashtyn had lost, and she was safe.

The Night of the Weeping Woman

Mary Kay Morel

J KNEW MOM wouldn't want me hanging around the Espanoza brothers, but when my classmate Louie threw a half-ripe tomato at my bedroom window, I was ready to slip off into the night with him and his big brother. Summers can be pretty slow in Cortina, and the Espanozas had a reputation for spicing things up. So when I heard that *thump,* I put on my jeans, cradled a flashlight under my arm, and took off.

"Hey, Bernardo, what's the flashlight for?" Elfrego, the older Espanoza, teased me as I crawled through the backyard fence. "Scared you'll see *La Llorona?*"

"Who's La Llorona?" I asked, pocketing my pencil-size light and ignoring his taunt.

"Some ghost story our grandma likes to tell," Elfrego said as we headed down the dark alley behind my house. "I thought everybody had heard of her."

"Well, I haven't," I sniffed, "and I've read a *lot* about ghosts."

So Louie and Elfrego told me the story of La Llorona, the Weeping Woman, who howled and shrieked and always wore white. They said she had been a real woman who lived long ago. One day her kids had disobeyed her and run off to the river. They drowned while playing there. When she found them in the water, she went crazy.

"Now the spirit of the Weeping Woman goes up and down the river's edge, looking for them," Elfrego explained in his best creature-feature voice. "Every time she sees a kid who doesn't do right, she cries and chases him because she mistakes him for her own."

"Grandma says if the Weeping Woman catches you, she'll snatch your soul," Louie added solemnly.

"Yeah, right. And pumpkins can fly," I scoffed.

"They can," Louie nodded excitedly, "if there's a witch in one. That's what my aunt Donita says."

"Aunt Donita's nuts," Elfrego cut in. "She also says La Llorona chased her once when she was playing with some kids under the old railroad bridge. Louie, you can't believe everything grownups say."

"Yeah, they just tell us these things to make us act better," I agreed.

Main Street wasn't much more than a few old buildings

falling apart. As soon as we got there, Elfrego headed for the Paradise Lounge and Bowling Alley. We ended up hanging around the Dumpsters in back so he could catch a glimpse of his dream girl, Kelly Karsen, the owner's daughter. Kelly worked in the kitchen. The fact that she was sixteen, two years older than Elfrego, didn't stop him from having a crush on her the size of South America.

"Let's go shoot some baskets up at the school," I suggested under my breath, but Louie wouldn't leave his big brother.

So we passed the time throwing rocks at a street lamp. Once Elfrego hid behind the Dumpster. He jumped out wrapped in some silly white towel he had found there. Then he started crying like a wounded cat, pretending to be La Llorona. I thought he acted dumb, but Louie looked scared. I guess those stories his grandma told had really gotten to him.

Finally, the big steel door in back swung open. We quieted down and hid. A guy stepped out. He was wearing a muscle shirt and an eagle tattoo. Elfrego looked startled. "Hey, that's Tony Murito," he muttered under his breath. "He's in Kelly's class at school."

We hung back in the shadows and watched. We noticed the big trash bag Tony carried. We noticed his bulgy biceps, too. He hoisted that load into the Dumpster the way a two-year-old lifts a pretend teapot. No effort at all. I couldn't help looking over at Elfrego's own scrawny biceps. Then we saw Kelly standing in the doorway, watching like she was ready to applaud.

"I told you she was too old for you," Louie said quietly after Big-Biceps Murito followed Kelly back inside.

Elfrego walked over and gave the Dumpster a kick. "Too bad La Llorona never caught Tony," he muttered, glaring at the closed kitchen door.

We were on Main Street when the last patron straggled out of the Paradise around midnight. Old Man Karsen locked up a few minutes later. Kelly had already left in the Bicep King's truck.

"Come on." Elfrego motioned us to follow. He'd picked up a tire iron back in the alley and was swinging it menacingly. "We're gonna break the front windows of the Paradise."

"Are you crazy?" Louie croaked in a froggy voice.

"They'll catch us," I said quickly. "Everybody knows you like Kelly. They'll figure it out if those windows get broke the same night she has a date with Tony."

"How do you know it was a date?" Elfrego asked, looking like he could kill me instead.

I ignored the question. "You don't want La Llorona chasing you because you broke Old Man Karsen's windows, do you?" I teased, trying to lighten that dark expression he wore.

Elfrego calmed down and dropped the tire iron. Then I noticed him looking at a car parked just off

Main Street, near Jim's Auto Repair. The front window on the driver's side was rolled down, and the key was hanging in the switch. He circled it the way a coyote looks at a rabbit he's about to have for lunch.

Finally, Elfrego popped his head inside, pulled the key out, and held it up for us to see. "Whoever left this in here is sure crazy." He laughed. "No, they weren't crazy," he changed his mind, "just dumb."

"Being dumb is not a crime. Stealing a car is." My voice sounded cool and steady, but my legs were shaking.

Elfrego dropped the key back onto the seat. "I'm not taking it," he said. "I'd rather steal Tony's truck."

We turned around, and Elfrego ducked behind the car. A few seconds later, he jumped up, still wrapped in that dumb towel, flapping his arms and making these noises like my grandma's creaky basement door.

"You sound stupid," I said with a grin. Actually it was nice to see him acting like the Weeping Woman again. That seemed harmless compared to stealing a car.

"Did I scare ya?" he asked. Then he motioned to the car. "Come on, let's have a real thrill. Let's at least go for a ride." I didn't figure Elfrego could actually drive, so I climbed in, thinking it wouldn't hurt to just sit in the car. It didn't even scare me when Elfrego started the engine.

"We won't get caught," he said, when he saw Louie and me looking at him. "We won't. We won't." Elfrego chanted these words over and over like some misguided prayer.

Suddenly his hand was on the gearshift, and we were moving. I expected the car to roll out of control and crash, right on Main Street. But it turned out Elfrego could drive pretty well. "My uncle's had me practicing since last summer," he bragged. "I bet I drive as good as Tony does."

Maybe. But I noticed Elfrego drove slower than Tony. Or even my grandma. We passed the last streetlight in town like some heavy bird winging its way toward the tropics. Elfrego crept southward over a dirt road that ran parallel with the river. Then suddenly he wasn't driving at all. The car's engine died, and we glided to a stop.

"What's wrong?" Louie yelled from the backseat.

"I don't know," Elfrego said with a frown. Then we noticed the gas needle, wriggling its finger on empty.

We climbed out of the car and left it parked along the road where it had stopped. I wondered if the cops would dust for fingerprints when they found it. I hoped not, but I'd seen enough crime shows on TV to worry that they might.

Then I smelled water. The river ran right below us. All we had to do was slide down a steep bank to reach it. "It will be safer following the river back into town," I said. "If we stay off the road, no one will suspect we stole that car."

"What about La Llorona?" Louie half whispered.

"Don't be a sissy," Elfrego ordered his brother. "Come on, guys," he motioned, marching down the bank like he was leading a battalion into war. "To the river."

The bank was steep. I fell twice. Once I scratched my arm, and it bled. I put my hand up to staunch the flow. Elfrego still had that stupid towel wrapped around his chest. It bobbed before me like a white light. "Take that thing off," I finally said. I don't know why, but the sight annoyed me.

Elfrego must have removed it, because suddenly I couldn't follow his bouncing form. Then I heard him yell, "Help! I'm caught! I'm caught! Something's got me."

"It's La Llorona!" Louie screamed. "She's got him!"

"Calm down," I shouted. Then I remembered the flashlight in my pocket. I dug it out fast and flashed it toward Elfrego's voice. There he stood, wrapped in a loop of stray fence wire.

"La Llorona, huh?" I bounced my light over on Louie, who winced sheepishly.

I had just finished unwrapping Elfrego when we heard the noise. It came from the water's edge. It sounded like something rustling through the brush down along the river. I figured it was an animal. Someone's stray cow. Or a coyote, maybe.

"It's just some rancher's dog," I said, hoping I was right.

Then came the howl. It shivered upward out of the throat of something not quite human. Something that lived on the dark side of midnight. Or the dark side of

the river. The sound slid over my skin like a witch's snake.

Then I saw her. She was coming toward us. I tried to make my feet move, but they wouldn't budge. I could only stare. At first she fluttered like a handkerchief, small and white. But the closer she came, the more she grew until she towered over us like a column of twisting, white smoke. Smoke with a face. And tears that fell from blank, empty eyes.

Her howl became a shriek, louder than the roar of floodwater. I realized the force of her by that sound. She was strong as the wind, solid as steel. If she reached us, she would turn us to dust.

"Run!" I screamed.

We scrambled up the bank, leaping clumps of rabbit-brush, dodging broken bottles and torn aluminum cans. Her shrieks and cries pummeled our ears as we zigzagged back toward the road. Once I thought I felt the chill of her smoke-skin brush my neck, but I didn't turn around. I was afraid she might be too close, those empty, weeping eyes peering down into my own as she reached out to snatch my soul.

When our feet hit the dirt road again, all noise stopped. The howl had let up in one great, shuddering gasp. We stood staring at each other, afraid to look back at the river, our eyes full of questions. Had we dreamed the Weeping Woman? Or had she been real? Had we found her back there along the water? Or had some dust devil freakishly spun down from the sky on this clear, quiet night?

"Maybe we just scared ourselves silly with all that talk of La Llorona," I finally said.

Elfrego shrugged and half nodded, but Louie didn't look convinced.

Slowly we turned around and looked back at the river, but it was a long, black snake that gave us no answer. We turned toward the road again, ready to walk to town and home to our mothers.

Then we heard it. One last howl that rose from the bottom of the dark water. There was our answer. The sound reached deep into my bones, turning them colder than gravestones.

But the howl sounded more sad than scary now. And it hung in that clear, quiet air like a mother's lonely question that could never be answered. Still, I was scared enough to know I wasn't going back to the river anytime soon. And I doubted I'd be going on any more joyrides in stolen cars with the Espanoza brothers.

The Man Who Sang to Ghosts

A Japanese Ghost Story

Aaron Shepard

"*T*ODAY'S BATTLE IS our last," the commander in chief told the men on the ship's deck. "Remember your honor and fight to the end. What more do we have to live for?"

No family in all Japan had held greater power than the Heike, or had risen to it so swiftly. But their fall had been even swifter. Chased from the capital city, they had been hounded by a rival clan for nearly two years. And now the remnant of the Heike and its loyal samurai warriors were arrayed in boats and ships off the coast at Dan-no-ura, ready for their final stand against the enemy fleet.

As arrows flew and swords whirled, as dead and wounded samurai fell in the boats or dropped into the sea, the doom of the Heike grew clear. Then it was that the clansmen, dressed

*in full armor, jumped into the waves, choosing to drown
themselves rather than fall into enemy hands.*

*One ship bore the child emperor and the court ladies.
When the emperor's grandmother saw that the end was near,
she took the emperor in her arms and declared, "Woman
though I am, I will not let the enemy lay hands on me. I will
go where the emperor must go."*

*"Where are you taking me, Grandmother?" asked the
puzzled boy.*

*Fighting tears, she told him, "Away from this world of
sorrow, to a happier one."*

And hugging him closely, she plunged into the sea.

The twanging notes of a *biwa* drifted over the temple
garden in the hot summer night.

Sitting cross-legged on the veranda, softly pluck-
ing the strings of the lute, was a blind young man
named Hoichi. He was dressed in the robe of a
Buddhist priest, and his head was shaved like one—
but he was not a priest. He was a bard, one of the
many blind bards who for centuries had kept alive the
tale of the Heike.

Sometime around midnight, unable to sleep in the
heat, Hoichi had come out into the evening air, with
his biwa to keep him company. As he played, he
thought about the weeks since coming to live at the
temple at Akama. How lucky he was that the priest
had invited him! He was just starting his career and
felt grateful he no longer had to worry about food or
lodging.

Then, too, there was the honor and thrill of residing in a temple so closely linked to the Heike. Dan-no-ura, the place of their final battle, was just at the edge of town. And it was to appease the restless Heike spirits that the townspeople had built this temple, along with a cemetery nearby, where the priest held services in front of Heike memorial tombs. As for the spirits themselves, they no longer caused too much trouble. But they still showed themselves on dark nights, appearing as small, ghostly flames that hovered over sea and sand. "Demon fires" they were called.

Hoichi's old teacher had told him, "To perform the tale of the Heike, you must know the Heike well." And where better to learn about them than in the temple at Akama?

Hearing something, Hoichi stopped his playing and listened. Through the night came footsteps, measured by a steady *clank, clank*—the sound of armor.

A samurai coming to the temple, thought Hoichi. What could he want at this hour?

The footsteps moved through the back gate and across the garden. *Clank, clank.* They were coming straight toward him! As the young man's heart beat faster, the footsteps halted before the veranda.

"Hoichi!"

"Sir!" replied the young man. Then he added, "Please, sir, I am blind. I cannot see who you are."

"You have nothing to fear," said the voice. "My master, a lord of high rank, is lodging nearby. He came to visit Dan-no-ura, the scene of the famous battle.

Now he hears of your talent in reciting the tale of the Heike and wishes you to come at once to perform for himself and his attendants."

"I am most honored," said Hoichi.

The young man slung his biwa on his back and slipped into his straw sandals. His arm was clasped in a grip of iron, and he was led rapidly out of the temple garden.

They started down the road to town, then turned toward the shore. Where could we be going? thought Hoichi. A great lord cannot stay on the beach!

But before they reached the beach, they stopped, and the samurai called, "Open!" The young man heard the sounds of a large double-doored gate swinging wide. How strange, thought Hoichi. I know nothing of a great house here.

They crossed a large yard, mounted some steps, removed their sandals, and passed through another door. The samurai led Hoichi down long walkways of polished wooden floors, around many corners, and across wide rooms carpeted with straw matting.

At last they entered what Hoichi could tell was a huge room filled with a great company. Silk robes rustled like leaves in a forest, and the air hummed with a multitude of soft voices.

Hoichi was led forward to a cushion on the floor, and the iron grip withdrew from his arm. The young man knelt and set down his biwa, then bowed to the lord he knew must be seated before him.

"Hoichi." The stern voice of an old woman came

from slightly to the left. The rest of the room fell silent. "You will now recite for us the tale of the Heike."

"It is my honor," said Hoichi, bowing again. "But the tale of the Heike takes many nights to perform in full. Which portion do you wish to hear tonight?"

There was a pause, and Hoichi sensed a tension in the room. Then a man's deep voice came from slightly to the right.

"Recite the tale of the Battle of Dan-no-ura. Of all tales, it is the most poignant."

Hoichi bowed once more, sat cross-legged, took up his biwa, and tuned it. Then, taking his large pick made of horn, he began to play.

Never had Hoichi played better. In the tones of his biwa were the roar of the sea, the whistling of arrows, the crashing of boats, the clanking of armor, the clanging of swords, the cries of fierce warriors.

And then Hoichi's voice lifted in chant. He sang of the gathering of forces at the scene of battle, the formal first exchange of arrows, the words of the commander in chief. He sang of the initial advances of the Heike, still hopeful, then the turning of the tide against them and the desertion of many supporters. He sang of the Heike clansmen holding fast to extra armor, even boat anchors, to speed their journey to the bottom of the sea.

At first the listeners were quiet, almost unnaturally so. But as the performance went on, they seemed to grow restless, anxious. Hoichi heard little exclamations, sounds of men weeping. Never have I affected an audience so deeply, thought Hoichi proudly. Encouraged, he performed even more brilliantly, even more movingly.

But as he began to sing of the emperor's grandmother—her taking the boy in her arms, the words she spoke to him—the cries and weeping grew louder, until Hoichi became uneasy. And when he sang of their leap into the waters, the company burst out in such wild wailing that Hoichi was frightened.

What has aroused them so? he wondered. Can my performance alone have done this?

Hoichi finished, and the noise in the room slowly subsided. Somewhere in front, a boy's quiet whimpering faded away.

"Hoichi," said the old woman, "we had heard high praise for your playing and reciting. But never did we imagine such skill as you have displayed. Our lord will remain here two more nights. You must come each night at the same hour and perform the tale again. And be assured, on the last night you will be well rewarded."

"Thank you!" said Hoichi, bowing again.

"But be warned," continued the woman. "Our lord does not wish his presence here known. Tell no one of your coming!"

The iron grip fell again on Hoichi's arm, and he was led quickly back the way he had come.

No one had seen Hoichi leave the temple. But the priest, returning after midnight from a service he had held, happened to enter by the back gate. He noticed that Hoichi's sandals were gone from the veranda steps, and checking inside, he found that the young man was not in his room.

Where could he be so late? he wondered.

The next morning, when the priest rose, he checked again and found Hoichi on his sleeping mat, snoring gently. Hours later, a servant reported that the young man was up at last, and the priest sent for him.

"Hoichi, you've worried me. You were out very late, and none of the servants knows anything about it. Why would you go out like that on your own?"

"It was nothing," said Hoichi. "Just a little business I had to attend to. Please don't concern yourself."

But the young man's answer worried the priest still more. It was not like Hoichi to be secretive.

Later he told one of the servants, "Keep a lookout tonight. If Hoichi leaves again, follow and see where he goes."

That night the servant kept watch on Hoichi's room from a far corner of the garden. Clouds covered the moon, and a light rain began to fall. The servant huddled under a tree, but the rain grew heavier.

"It's almost midnight," grumbled the man. "He won't leave so late, and not in this rain! I'm going to bed."

Just then he saw Hoichi come out of his room with his biwa and sit on the covered veranda. "What's he up to?" mumbled the servant.

Hoichi sat for a long time, softly playing the lute. Then he stopped and seemed to listen to something. All at once, he stiffened and called out, "Sir!"

The puzzled servant looked around. "Who does he think he's talking to?"

He saw Hoichi rise, sling his biwa on his back, slip into his sandals, and come down the steps. The bard did not seem to notice the rain. Walking more briskly than a blind man should, he crossed the garden and passed through the gate.

The servant rushed inside and grabbed a lantern. By the time he got out to the road, Hoichi was already out of sight, and the rain was falling in sheets.

"Hoichi! Hoichi!" The servant hurried toward town, expecting to catch up any minute. But he didn't see a soul.

"How could he move so quickly? I'd better find him, or the priest will be furious!"

When the servant reached town, he knocked on the doors of every house and establishment he could remember the young man visiting. But all he got for his efforts were the curses of those he awakened.

"It's no use," he told himself. "I've tried everywhere."

He started back to the temple, walking this time by way of the shore. Suddenly, amid the howling of the wind and the beating of the rain, he heard the tones of a biwa and a voice raised in chant.

"It's Hoichi!" he cried and hurried toward the sounds.

*   *   *

Once more Hoichi sat in the great hall. Once more his
biwa and his voice brought to life the Battle of Dan-
no-ura. Once more came the little outbursts, the
sounds of weeping, growing louder, more anguished,
more fervent, until—

"Hoichi!"

What's this? thought Hoichi. It sounds like one of
the temple servants! But what is he doing here? And
how could he think of interrupting me?

Hoichi kept playing, kept singing. The emperor's
grandmother, taking the boy in her arms, stepping to
the edge of the ship. . . .

"Hoichi! Hoichi!"

The voice was in his ear, and a hand was on his
shoulder, shaking him.

The listeners in the room had grown strangely
quiet. Hoichi, still playing his biwa, said in a low,
desperate voice, "Are you out of your mind? I am performing for this noble company. Go away or you will
bring disaster on us both!"

"Hoichi, you are bewitched! There is no noble
company. You are sitting in the rain, here in the cemetery of the Heike. In front of you are the memorial
tombs of the emperor, his grandmother, and the commander in chief. And all around you are hundreds of
demon fires!"

"What are you talking about?" said Hoichi. "I am
in a palace, performing for a great lord!"

The servant did not argue further. Much bigger

than Hoichi, he slipped an arm across the young man's chest and hauled him off the muddy ground.

"Stop!" cried Hoichi, struggling. "Please! Leave me alone! You'll ruin everything!"

Ignoring both pleading and struggling, the servant dragged Hoichi toward the cemetery gate.

The priest looked with concern on the pale, downcast figure before him.

"Hoichi, I'm glad you have finally trusted me enough to explain yourself. And I hope you now understand that it was not for a great lord you performed the tale of the Heike, but for the spirits of the Heike themselves."

"I understand," said Hoichi softly.

"Good," said the priest. "Then you should also understand that if you return, the only reward they will give you will be to tear your body to pieces—to give you the honor of joining them forever. You are in great danger, my friend, for the samurai will surely come again this third night."

The young man trembled.

"None of us here," said the priest, "can oppose this ghostly warrior. But I have thought of a way to save you. It will require great courage and strength of will. Are you willing to try?"

"I am," said Hoichi.

At the priest's request, the young man stripped off his clothes. Then the priest took a brush and ink and began to write on Hoichi's body.

"I am inscribing on you a passage from sacred scripture. When the holy text covers every part of your body—from the top of your head to the soles of your feet—you will be invisible to the spirits. Tonight, when the samurai calls you, sit still and do not make a sound. He will not be able to find you. When he leaves, you'll be free from danger for good."

At last the priest finished writing. "I'm afraid I must hurry out to hold a service in a nearby village. I won't be back till very late, but if you do just as I have told you, you'll be perfectly safe. Good luck, my friend."

That night, a little before midnight, Hoichi stepped from his room and sat on the veranda. His biwa lay in his lap, but he did not play it. He sat still, trying to calm the beat of his heart.

At last he heard it—*clank, clank.* Through the back gate—*clank, clank.* Across the garden—*clank, clank.* Before the veranda—*clank.*

"Hoichi!"

The young man caught his breath and forced himself not to reply.

"Hoichi!!"

He tried to stop shaking.

"Hoichi!!!"

His hands clenched as he willed himself not to faint.

"H'm," said the voice in front of him. "I see the biwa. But of the bard I see nothing."

The footsteps moved onto the veranda and circled partway around him.

"Nothing, that is, except two ears."

Two ears? How can he see my ears? thought Hoichi.

The steps moved directly behind him. "A bard with no hands or mouth will hardly serve my lord. Still, I must show I have followed orders as best I can. I had better take the ears."

Hoichi froze in terror. He felt two hands clamp his ears in an iron grip and . . .

Later that night the priest returned from the nearby village. Anxious about Hoichi, he entered by the back gate and crossed the garden. Then he stopped in horror.

"Hoichi!" he cried. He rushed to the veranda. "My dear friend, what have they done?"

There lay the bard, still and silent, his head resting in a pool of blood.

He was alive, but barely. The priest himself bandaged the wounds and sat all night by the young man's mat.

It was late morning before Hoichi stirred. Almost at once, he reached up to the sides of his head and touched the cloth winding over and around.

The eyes of the priest filled with tears. "My friend, I'm so sorry. It was all my fault, my terrible, terrible fault. I thought I had covered your body completely with the sacred writing. But in my haste to leave, I forgot to write on your ears!"

*   *   *

Hoichi recovered and, as time went on, prospered as well. Word of his adventure spread, and many curious lords and ladies traveled great distances to hear him play and recite. And so he gained both fame and wealth.

What's more, Hoichi's encounter gave his performance a depth and power achieved by few others. For, as his teacher had once said, "To perform the tale of the Heike, you must know the Heike well."

And who could know them better than the man called Hoichi the Earless?

Author Biographies

Deepa Agarwal is the author of more than twenty-five children's books published in both English and Hindi. These include picture books, folk tales, ghost stories, mysteries, adventure stories, and biographies. She is also a regular contributor to many children's periodicals. Ms. Agarwal lives in India.

Gerry Armstrong (1938–1999) was the author of an award-winning trilogy of children's books on Celtic themes: *The Magic Bagpipe, The Boat on the Hill,* and *The Fairy Thorn.* She also published short stories in various anthologies and magazines for children. She was an avid storyteller and folk singer in the Chicago area, where she entertained groups of school-children for over twenty years.

Marion Dane Bauer is the author of more than twenty-five books for young people, from picture books and easy readers to novels. She has won numerous awards, including a Jane Addams Peace Association Award for her novel *Rain of Fire* and a Newbery Honor for another novel, *On My Honor.* Her books have been translated into more than a dozen languages.

Robert Culp's first publication was a poem at age twelve, and since then he has published many children's stories and articles, including several in *Cricket*. A handful of his short stories have appeared in other literary magazines. He is a professor of aerospace engineering at the University of Colorado, where he is chair of the department.

Frank Dodge began writing short stories just before turning seventy. Since then he's been published all over the world, including Iceland and Russia. A veteran of World War II, the Korean War, and the Vietnam War, he lives in Louisiana.

Nancy Etchemendy lives in the San Francisco Bay area with her husband, John, and their son, Max. She is the author of a number of short stories and several books for children, including *The Power of Un*. "Bigger than Death" earned her a Bram Stoker Award in 1999.

Since her award-winning picture book *Jamaica's Find* was published, **Juanita Havill** has written four more books about Jamaica and her family and friends. She has also written middle-grade novels, early chapter books, and letters to every reader who wrote to her about "The Mysterious Girl at the Pool" when the story appeared in *Cricket*.

Twenty-seven years ago a librarian friend showed **Eric A. Kimmel** a new children's magazine called *Cricket*. "I'd like to write for that!" he exclaimed.

His first stories appeared in some of *Cricket*'s earliest issues. Since then he has published over fifty books, including the ever-popular *Anansi and the Moss-Covered Rock* and a Caldecott Honor book, *Hershel and the Hanukkah Goblins,* which originally appeared in *Cricket.* Dr. Kimmel is professor emeritus of education at Portland State University. He and his wife, Doris, live in Portland, Oregon.

Mary Kay Morel's articles and stories for young readers and adults have appeared in many publications, including *Cricket* and *Spider.* She lives in Colorado.

Kathleen M. Muldoon is a freelance writer of children's literature. Her work has appeared in *Cricket* and many other children's magazines. She is also the author of a picture book, *Princess Pooh.* She and her cat, Prissy, live in San Antonio, Texas.

Susan Price is the award-winning author of the trilogy *Ghost Drum, Ghost Song,* and *Ghost Dance,* as well as a short story collection, *Nightcomers.* She lives in England.

Aaron Shepard is the author of *Master Man, The Sea King's Daughter, The Baker's Dozen,* and many other picture books, as well as numerous stories in *Cricket.* His retellings of folk tales and other traditional literature have been honored by the American Library

Association, the National Council for Social Studies, and the American Folklore Society. He lives in California.

Josepha Sherman is a fantasy writer and folklorist who has written more than thirty books and one hundred short stories for children and adults. Her titles range from *Merlin's Kin: World Tales of the Heroic Magician* to *Star Trek: Vulcan's Heart.* She was a winner of the Compton Crook Award for Best Fantasy Novel. Ms. Sherman lives in New York.